a rabbit's tale

a rabbit's tale

JOHN WILDE

NPI

Northwest Publishing, Inc.
Salt Lake City, Utah

A Rabbit's Tale

All rights reserved.
Copyright © 1995 Northwest Publishing, Inc.

Reproduction in any manner, in whole or in part,
in English or in other languages, or otherwise
without written permission of the publisher is prohibited.

This is a work of fiction.
All characters and events portrayed in this book are fictional,
and any resemblance to real people or incidents is purely coincidental.

For information address: Northwest Publishing, Inc.
6906 South 300 West, Salt Lake City, Utah 84047
J. B. 2-22-95
Edited by: C. D. Allen

PRINTING HISTORY
First Printing 1995

ISBN: 1-56901-488-4

NPI books are published by Northwest Publishing, Incorporated,
6906 South 300 West, Salt Lake City, Utah 84047.
The name "NPI" and the "NPI" logo are trademarks belonging to
Northwest Publishing, Incorporated.

PRINTED IN THE UNITED STATES OF AMERICA.
10 9 8 7 6 5 4 3 2 1

*To my father, Mit Wilde, who gave
me his love of the outdoors and its wonder.*

*To my mother, Jeanne Wilde,
who gave me my love of stories.*

*And to my own warren: Joann, John, Heather,
Megan, and Rachel, who listened to my tales
with interest on many a long trip and
allowed me the time and solitude
needed to write, so the stories
they grew to love could be
shared with others.*

1
the legend of the birth

There are many legends of his birth. Today no one can say with certainty which are true and which are not. If we take a compilation of the stories most told on long winter days by the elders it would go something like this: It was late in the fall, during a severe, early snow storm, that the doe arrived. She crawled to the mouth of the warren, more dead than alive, and very heavy with child. The clan did all they could to nurture her, but on that same day of the storm, her babies were born. Legend has it that six kits were born, but of the six, only the first born survived. Both the doe and the rest of her offspring died during the birthing.

The sole survivor of the disaster was a buck, and even as a newborn, he looked different. Most striking were his ears.

Unlike normal kits', his ears lay down and could only be raised with obvious effort. For an animal that lives by hearing and fleeing from danger, this deformity was considered an ominous sign by all the clan.

And then there were the kit's legs. All four appendages were longer than those of any rabbit ever seen by the clan. Even the claws were different—larger, sharper looking, and disturbingly unrabbitlike. The combination of a severe storm so early, the miraculous appearance from seemingly nowhere by the doe, the deaths that followed, and the birth of the strangely deformed kit had the whole warren, who were a most superstitious group at any time, in a buzz of excitement laced with fear.

The Lord Rabbit had to be consulted at once, of course, but he was very old, weak, and feeble. The violent storm had done nothing to help his condition. A long discussion took place among the warren members as to how to best proceed. Suddenly an old doe named Rachel, long without kits of her own, simply picked up the newborn with her teeth and hopped gently down the tunnel to the Lord's chambers.

Of course, the guard rabbits at the entrance to the Lord's den stopped her at once. They would have driven her away, but defying generations of rabbit tradition, Rachel let out the scream of pain. This is the one verbal signal all rabbits can make—a sharp, shrill, horrifying sound. This cry is usually heard only from an animal in extreme pain or terror, or in the grip of death's final bite. Never is it uttered within the warren itself. The guards were shocked, then grew angry. They would have punished her on the spot, but the old Lord called for her to be allowed to enter.

No one witnessed this meeting that would forever change the lives of the entire warren. The Lord afterward fell into a deep sleep and died quickly. We have only Rachel's account to base our history on, so base it on that we must. The legend has been so oft told as to certainly have been altered from the truth, but the following is a well-intended story of that fateful encounter.

Rachel spoke. "My Lord, I apologize for the disturbance. You know me, and only a matter of great import would lead to such behavior on my part."

"Rachel, my dear, is that you? Come close and tell me what troubles you so to bring forth the scream."

Rachel approached and lay the new kit at the Lord's feet. As he slowly realized what he was seeing, she explained the strange events that surrounded the birth.

Carefully the ancient Lord studied the new one. Gently he touched the malformed and troubling ears. He noted the misshapen legs and claws as he heard the tale of its strange and tragic birth. The story told, he leaned back with a sigh.

"Rachel, my old friend, you know the laws of the clan. No rabbit born so deformed can live with us. He must be taken to the forest edge at once and set out. The Creator will take him back to himself, and a new, perfect kit will be born in his place."

"My Lord, never have I questioned the law, even with a kit of my own. But…can you not feel it?"

The old Lord was silent for so long, Rachel feared he had begun the great journey to join his ancient ancestors. At length he stirred. Since the strange kit had entered his chamber, he too had felt it. There was a force, of what kind neither of them could say, yet both were aware of its presence. The sad, misshapen body spoke of evil, yet the force seemed to contain none. The Lord knew he was close to his final journey. Maybe he felt too close to set this infant out. Setting deformed infants out on the forest edge was a painful task he had been forced all too often to perform.

"The kit can remain until spring. Rachel, it must stay with you. When the snows are gone, it will be turned away. May the Great Rabbit protect it."

The verdict was sealed in traditional form, by the naming of the kit. The Lord stared long into its tiny but clear eyes. He studied again the malformed ears that would mean sure and early death to a rabbit who couldn't hear the light footfalls of a fox or sense the currents caused by the wingbeats of a hawk.

"The child shall be called Ulys," spoke the old Lord, and he turned his back. Maybe the sound of the storm muffled his words. Maybe Rachel's years blurred her hearing. No such name had ever been spoken in the history of the warren.

Rachel sat patiently until it was clear no more was forthcoming from her Lord. She left and told the incredulous scribe stationed at the Lord's door to record the incredible name. The name recorded in the book of the warren certified Ulys's existence and guaranteed his protection within the warren.

One final strange part of the legend exists. Hours later, after the Lord had begun his final journey, he was discovered with a gentle smile on his face.

2
young ulys

Rachel hurried with her precious burden to her small, lonely, bare den at the back of the warren. She had long been alone and was filled with joy at the chance to aid a life, even one as tragically begun as that of tiny Ulys. She kept the infant sequestered from all the rest of the warren, leaving him only to obtain food for them both. She chewed grass to a finely ground pulp and fed it to Ulys from her own lips. As the days passed, the kit grew. He began to move easily around the tiny room, but the sad ears remained cast down.

As soon as the kit was old enough to understand her efforts, Rachel began to work with his ears. She held them up as long as her forepaws were able, but they collapsed in the same horizontal heap when released. As Ulys got older, he could hold them erect himself, but only for a few moments, and then with great effort. Finally both Rachel and Ulys realized that the ears were shaped forever in this recumbent position, so strange for rabbits, and reluctantly accepted their form as the Creator's will.

Rachel realized that, malformed ears or no, Ulys had to meet the rest of the warren. It was a sad and fearful day when she summoned all of her strength and took the baby out to the common feeding grounds.

By now it was the dead of winter, and the rabbits all labored greatly to dig up a little nourishment from the grip of ice and snow. Several weeks had passed since Ulys's arrival, and the first sight of the newest member of the warren was a shock. Soon the shock gave way to anger. These were the months of death. Predators paroled the areas around the warren's mouth night and day. To be forced to stray a few feet farther from the protection of the warren's mouth to find sustenance could mean death to any member of the clan. Yet, here was this creature feeding among them and eating of their small but vital food supply.

When that day's feeding ended and the rabbits returned to the warmth of the big meeting room, the shock of seeing Ulys soon turned to cruelty. Poor Rachel could do nothing but watch as Ulys was taunted and bitten by other warren members. It was true, he had grown much since his strange arrival, but with his weird hop and misshapen features, he could do little to protect himself against the other, larger rabbits.

The look of pain and incomprehension on Ulys's face tore Rachel's heart. She knew this was a passage he had to go through, but she had never before seen a rabbit treated so cruelly. As she silently and sadly watched, a young buck had Ulys cornered and wouldn't let him pass. The poor kit was battered and terrified. Facing the wall in a feeble attempt to avoid some of the blows, he was bitten and swatted repeatedly. In desperation Ulys did something never before seen by any rabbit in the warren.

Rising on his long forelegs, little Ulys kicked backward with his even longer back legs. He caught his tormentor completely off guard and drove him tumbling and falling to the other side of the room. The shaken buck arose with a yelp. The strange claws had punctured his skin in several places. The other rabbits retreated, and Rachel and Ulys took advantage of the confusion to move back to their den. Ulys wasn't badly hurt, but the look on his young face was one of shock and horror. It would be a long time before that look would leave.

The other rabbits were stunned by what they had seen. Rabbits didn't fight. Their protection, given by the Great Rabbit, was in their senses of hearing, smell, and vision that allowed them to detect danger, and then their quick hind-leg kick that allowed them to escape. When caught by a predator, rabbits simply died. In the rare battles between rabbits themselves, their weapons were their teeth and, to some extent, their short, weak front claws. It was as strange for them to witness Ulys's powerful hind-leg kick as it would have been to have seen a rabbit in a fight who suddenly flew away.

From then on, Ulys fed every day with the warren. None sought to hurt him, as they saw what he had done to his much larger adversary. Yet neither did any befriend him. He fed in the farthermost spot possible from the warren's mouth and thus from its safety. None of the other rabbits would even look his way, except for the young buck he had kicked in that memorable first meeting. This buck, named Duke, was seen to stare often at young Ulys. But the meaning of the look he gave Ulys was impossible to interpret.

At the far edge of the feeding circle, Ulys found the best food. Old and slow, Rachel didn't dare feed so far from the safety of the mouth, but Ulys would return to her with the best of what he found. He was growing at a rate unheard of for a rabbit in the winter, but the deformed ears never moved.

One strange fact may have kept Ulys from being driven from the warren and to his death by the clan. All winter long, since Ulys had joined them, not one predator had been seen.

As their natural fear of moving from the mouth of the warren slowly decreased, the rabbits were able to find more and better food, and thus grow in strength and spirits. This unusual peace and quiet during the months of death made the clan upbeat and gay as the long winter days slowly ebbed away.

3
ulys learns

Rachel had lived for many seasons in the warren. She knew as much about the secrets of life in the den as any rabbit ever had, including the Lord Rabbits. She reflected deeply as to how she could best help this gentle, strange buck the Great Rabbit had blessed and entrusted her with in her old age.

Nothing she could do or say would make the other rabbits accept this strange-looking creature as one of their own. Since that first tremulous day in the great hall, she and Ulys had done their best to remain isolated within the circle of the warren. To become involved in conflict could result in being driven into the winter cold to certain death. The new Lord Rabbit was much younger than Rachel and she couldn't predict how he would react to Ulys if she approached him. Long years had taught her that rather than risk a confrontation, it was better for the two of them to remain alone and stay out of the way.

To pass the long hours in their small den together, Rachel told the young buck tales. Rachel was a gifted storyteller, the most sought after of all the members of the clan. All the ancient lore of the rabbit clan was told and retold on long winter days. Ulys would never tire of hearing the tales. The adventures of the heroes of the warren's past and stories of the Great Rabbit made his eyes burn bright with intensity and joy. But Rachel knew much more than legends would be required if Ulys was to survive. In the dark of winter she told Ulys all she knew of the outdoors: tales of the habits of hawk, fox, and wolf, and of the locations of secret caves and springs. The vast storehouse of her knowledge, gathered over a long lifetime, she poured into her eager pupil. No rabbit ever listened with such interest and intensity as Ulys did.

And never did Ulys receive enough. His questions led her to discover things she wasn't aware she knew. The signs she knew given by air, water, and land became his. As Ulys fed at increasingly greater distances from the mouth, he began to discover how the wood lore that Rachel had taught him in the safety of their den worked in the real world. He learned even more with his own observations.

During the feeding times, as Ulys strayed farther and farther from the mouth, the other warren members would look on with horror, yet with admiration for his daring. Even the guard rabbits were afraid to venture out to call him back. Yet day after day he returned safely, and daily he grew. Soon he was the tallest rabbit in the warren.

Though the others lacked the courage to stray so far, they envied him and Rachel the delectable morsels Ulys found in his travels. As the winter season lengthened, it took great courage for the other members of the clan, pushed by their growing hunger, to venture far enough from the mouth to find enough food to merely survive. All knew that, in this season, the predators grew lean and hungry, too.

But it wasn't just food Ulys sought as his feeding paths lengthened. Three things led him far from safety: a burning desire to learn and experience what Rachel told him of the woods, a stronger desire for moments of peace away from his tormentors, and the thrill of being the lone rabbit brave enough to venture so far. As he satisfied these goals, he grew in strength, confidence, and courage. The hard lonely life, forced on him by a cruel fate, was creating a creature never seen in the warren before.

4
ulys grows strong

In addition to the rabbit legends Rachel related and the carefully thought-out lessons on woodland lore, the days were filled with hard work. Rachel feared that one day she would be forced to choose between abandoning Ulys or leaving the warren. Old and weak as she was, her love for Ulys left no doubt what that choice would be, even it meant death for them both. Witnessing the frantic kick given to Duke in the common room by a young and terrified Ulys had made her realize that his odd form of rabbit behavior could offer some advantage. In the dark of their den, hidden from the eyes of the others in the warren, Ulys spent hours building strength in those long legs with excrcise.

In the beginning these exercises had been only a game.

Rachel would make a mark on the den wall and Ulys would try to jump and touch it. Soon the ceiling had to be further dug out to accommodate Ulys's increasing size, as well as his incredible leaping ability. Before long, Rachel was unable to reach high enough to mark a goal that Ulys couldn't easily reach.

The exercise was enjoyable, yet strange and unique. All the kits exercised and played in the large common room, both for their amusement and to increase their strength for when spring came and released them from winter's grip. They would then venture beyond their dens and into the outer world. The other members of the clan ran races and played games of long jump with each other, but no rabbit jumped upward, only outward. It was this horizontal jump that created the quickness and speed needed to flee from any predators. The vertical jumping game was forced on Ulys by the cramped quarters where he and Rachel had sequestered themselves.

All hope of normal, upright rabbit ears had been abandoned long ago, but to her surprise, Rachel found Ulys's hearing to be excellent. Every day they worked to train both his ears and his other senses to detect the slightest of warnings. Soon Ulys could hear an earthworm digging deep below, in the cold earth.

To further expand their den, Ulys had instinctively begun to balance on his front paws and kick with his long back legs against the ceiling and walls. As the ceiling was thus excavated, his ability to jump in this unorthodox and decidedly unrabbitlike manner was developed.

All these activities were kept a complete secret from the other clan members. Certainly the dirt being removed and the strange sounds of the practice exercise were noticed, but living together all winter long in the cramped warren had taught the rabbits to respect each other's privacy, and even the most nosy of the clan would never dream of spying on another member's actions. Such spying in the forced close winter quarters was a social taboo that even the guard rabbits didn't break.

As the months passed, Rachel noticed some incredible changes in young Ulys. Maybe they were caused by better food, possibly by the unusual exercises, or maybe even by something related to the long, deformed legs. Whatever the explanation, the power of those four gangly extremities was awesome. The kicks done during exercise and play literally shook the earth and knocked more dirt from their den's ceiling.

Yet, despite the rare good fortune of Ulys finding plenty of good food to eat in the season of death and the visible growth in height and power of Ulys, Rachel still worried long into many sleepless winter nights. Rabbits are social animals, as befits their existence in a common warren. But Rachel spoke to few of her old friends, and Ulys spoke to no one. As they passed through the common room, Rachel could see the hurt in the now huge buck's eyes. This same hurt would become the energy that drove him to great lengths in his exercise. But while the exercises exorcised some of the pain, much of it remained.

5
ulys the warrior

    The day began normally enough. The weather showed signs of an early spring. What snow remained was so light as to no longer hinder the rabbits' feeding. Maybe being able to see the new green and tender growth more easily explains what happened. Maybe the guard rabbits and all the rest of the clan grew lax due to the length of time since the last predator attack. Maybe it was just bad luck.

    Megan was a young doe, born just before Ulys appeared in the warren. She was cute and friendly, well liked by all the rabbits of the warren, young and old alike. Rachel had seen her at times staring at her and Ulys as they made their lonely way through the common room to their den, but like all of the other rabbits, Megan had never spoken to either of them.

This warm early spring morning, Megan had wandered too far from the safety of the warren. About one hundred yards from the mouth, near a large bush, some new grass growth could be seen. After a long winter of eating dry grass, the temptation was too much for the young doe to resist.

When the fox sprang from the bush and grabbed Megan, there was hardly a sound. Rabbits flee, not fight. They fled. Once in the teeth of the fox, nothing is left for them to do but prepare to meet the Great Rabbit and offer up a death cry.

The other rabbits heard the sudden movement of the fox and fled for the mouth of the warren. In seconds, nothing remained of the scene except the fox, calmly walking toward its den with Megan held firmly between its teeth by the scruff of her neck.

As the fox leisurely passed the bush, recently its hiding place, the foliage seemed to erupt, as if shaken by a violent wind. The fox, seemingly affected by the same wind, tumbled over the ground while Megan went flying. Suddenly Ulys appeared from deep within the bush and pushed the stunned Megan to the safety of the mouth of the warren. Once inside, he left Megan to the care of the amazed clan, who looked at her as if she were a spirit. Other than a few scratches and bumps, Megan was unhurt. Ulys returned to Rachel and their den. Once again, Rachel was left to contemplate in wonder the behavior of this unique creature she had come to love as her own.

6
the legend of the great rabbit

This is the story most requested by young rabbits on winter nights in the warren. It both summarizes and explains the philosophy of life held by the rabbits. It is the story of the creation of the world and the part that rabbits played in this great event.

When the Creator, or the Great One, first made the world, all the creatures existed in harmony. They lived in peace in the same fields and played together daily. However, in time, many of the other animals grew to dislike the Great Rabbit, because in games of skill, speed, and daring, he often won. And when he won, he had such great joy!

The fact that the Great Rabbit loved to joke and play tricks didn't help his popularity with the other members of the animal kingdom. It seemed the rabbit was unable (or unwilling) to control his urge to play little games, too often at his friends' expense.

The happy lives of common bliss among all the animals of the earthly kingdom ended, due to the rabbit and his penchant for jokes. It seemed the God of Creation was also fond of games, but preferred to watch rather than to play. He admired the rabbit for his skill and daring, and with this esteem the Creator made the rabbit even more bold.

One day the rabbit decided it would be great fun to play a trick on the Great One, himself. Typical of the rabbit's jests, this one was intended to be harmless. The Great One carried with him at all times a large staff. He rarely spoke without first rising and holding the staff aloft. The rabbit felt it would be great fun to *borrow* the staff for a short while.

As a day of games and feasting was due, the rabbit waited until all the others were either engaged in the races or closely watching the events. As softly as a breeze, he crept up behind the Great One. The rabbit had great strength and was much larger than today's earthly version of the creature. He easily lifted the staff and stole quietly away.

The jester rabbit didn't know that what he took, in such a light moment, was indeed the staff of life. He had gone only a few feet when the sky turned black, and even the Great One cried out in fear. The terrified rabbit retraced his steps and soon restored the staff to the Great One, and thus light to the skies. As soon as the other animals recovered their wits and courage, they demanded to know what had happened.

The Great One knew what had been done and by whom. When he explained, the other animals all demanded the rabbit be put to death. His joke had almost resulted in the destruction of the world. Such examples of foolishness by the rabbit had become dangerous and had to be stopped.

The Great One was sad. He knew the other animals were right. Such behavior could not be tolerated, yet he loved the rabbit most for the very skill and daring the trick had required.

At last, he arose and held his staff aloft. All the animals grew quiet.

"The rabbit has done a terrible thing," the Creator proclaimed. "Indeed, he must be punished. From now until the end of time his front legs will be small and weak. He will be forced to flee from all the animals of the world, for he will be their favorite food. They will hunt him down without mercy and devour him."

The other animals would have set upon the rabbit then, thus finishing the story, but again the staff was raised. "I give these gifts to the rabbit to help him in this terrible plight. He will be fruitful and bear many young, so never will his enemies destroy all rabbits from the earth. I also grant him strong back legs to flee from danger, and large ears with which he can hear his predators' approach."

With that, the staff was lowered, and the rabbit leaped from the heavens with such daring quickness that none of his enemies could follow his path to earth.

What the Great One foretold became true. Many are those who feed on the rabbit, and thus great is his trouble, yet the Great One's blessings have always kept rabbits from being destroyed by all their mighty enemies.

This is the greatest of all rabbit legends. It explains who rabbits are and why they exist. It also explains why they accept death at the hands of their enemies with no struggle. It is simply their fate as decreed long ago by the Great One.

No rabbit in the long history of the warren had ever fought to escape. They were blessed with great vision, hearing, and sense of smell. When they sensed danger, they ran like the wind to safety. If they didn't reach shelter in time, they offered a death cry and knew they would be sent again to the earth by the Great Rabbit.

When the shock of Ulys's deed had worn off, the rabbits met in council. There was a strong division in feeling about what had happened. Some, mainly the young, felt this was a deed of great courage and should be rewarded with honors.

Others felt that Ulys's action had been almost a sin. It had gone against the creed rabbits had forever lived by. Such actions should not and could not have been tolerated.

Ulys himself had no idea why he had acted as he had. It was just a combination of where he happened to be (in the fox's path) and his reaction to the look of terror and pain on Megan's face. Maybe he had felt pain too often himself to just accept it. Whatever the reason, he had simply reacted, putting his hours of training to good use.

Among Megan and her family, no controversy existed. All loved Megan greatly and were grateful beyond their ability to express that Ulys had acted to save her. Her big brother, Buck, (of the now-famous, common-room kick) led the group of family members to Rachel and Ulys's den.

Buck scratched gently at the wall outside the den. When Rachel and Ulys stepped out, no one spoke. After a long silence, Buck simply asked Ulys if he would care to join the family in some games of celebration. Ulys said that he would. Quietly Megan came forward and touched noses with Ulys. For the first moment since Ulys's arrival in the warren, Rachel saw a gleam in the young buck's eye that was completely free of pain and fear.

7
chatter

The new acceptance by at least part of the clan made Rachel and Ulys glad. Rachel especially was delighted, as she alone knew of the old Lord's final pronouncement, the same as law among the clan, that Ulys must leave the warren in the fast-approaching spring season. She was very aware that sometime soon the support of other members of the clan might be critical to their well-being.

Ulys was just glad to be included in the others' activities. He still spent most of his time with Rachel, exercising and trying to absorb all he could from her wonderful storehouse of wisdom. He sensed the other rabbits' distrust of him. But the positive change in his status with some in the clan made him reflect. Why was he so distrusted? Certainly it was not due to any act of his.

Was he punished simply for the way he looked? Had not the Great Rabbit, in his wisdom, created him as he was? Was it true that rabbits must accept whatever came, even violent death, as simply their fate and not dare to struggle against it? None of the legends of the Great Rabbit that Rachel had so lovingly told him made him feel this humble acceptance of death was the Great Rabbit's desire for his children, nor the path he would have chosen himself.

Such thoughts no rabbit dared to express. The close life of the warren made it essential that all live in harmony. Any questions such as these, if raised at all, were answered by the Lord Rabbit, and his word was obeyed. Could it be that all the clan was wrong? Such a thought was too outlandish to give credence to.

Still, spring and the old Lord's commanded expulsion of Ulys grew ever closer. As the foliage grew, the rabbits were afforded more protection by the growth and could venture farther from the mouth of the warren to eat and play. Soon, it was only after dark that they met in the common room, and then just to sleep. No son or daughter of the Great Rabbit would choose the dark common room over a chance to be outside in the spring, despite the danger. Their love of the outdoors was too great.

Ulys loved his new-found freedom. Being outdoors, even if he was alone, didn't seem to be as lonely as being in the warren, surrounded by rabbits, with no one to talk to. Buck, Megan, and their family went out of their way to include him in their activities, but most of the other warren members, if they no longer attacked him, made it clear they didn't relish his company.

It was on one of these lonely journeys, away from the warren and the safety of the mouth, that Ulys's fate was again to take a dramatic turn.

It was a beautiful spring morning when, mostly due to chance and random wandering (and aided somewhat by the enticing smell of the apple blossoms), Ulys hopped up the hill to the grove of apple trees. He was enjoying nibbling a few low-hanging buds from the trees and learning the new smells, when his keen ear heard sounds in one of the apple trees. Unable to tell exactly where the noise came from, Ulys froze completely still, all his senses on maximum alert.

He knew the sounds were not from a bird. He had seen many of them and could quickly and easily identify the hawk and eagle. His ears tracked the noise to a movement in the leaves near the top of an old apple tree. Finally, he saw the furry creature that had so alarmed him. It jumped gracefully to the next tree, then sensed Ulys's presence. Instead of freezing as a rabbit would, it let out a piercing stream of chatter.

From the chatter, Ulys realized this was the squirrel Rachel had told him of. A colony of them lived in the hickory trees near the apple grove. He knew they were no threat to him, but he was fascinated by the squirrel's lack of fear. Slowly, he approached the tree until he was directly under the squirrel.

"Well, aren't you the brave one," said the squirrel. "Why don't you run and hide like all the rest of your kind? And what's wrong with your ears? Are they broken?" asked the squirrel.

"Why don't you run from other animals?" asked Ulys. "Why do you show no fear?" Such unnatural behavior as not running from danger was incomprehensible to him.

"I fear none on the ground because I can climb a tree. Only the birds of prey and man hold danger for me."

Ulys thought of the freedom such an ability would give. To rise above the earth—the earth that was the shelter and home of his kind—was an idea that would never have entered his mind. Climbing a tree was as foreign to the rabbit's nature as living underwater would be. And yet...the freedom! As he thought, the idea seemed to him to be almost like an escape from death—as wild an experience as Megan's drop from the jaws of the fox.

"How can you do such a thing? How can one climb into the sky?" asked Ulys.

"I was born in a tree," said the squirrel, with no little amusement at the foolishness of the query. "Climbing holds for me no mystery. Maybe with some help from me, you can learn too."

And as simply as that, a friendship that would change forever the lives of both of these creatures, and all those who knew them, was born.

With great wisdom, the squirrel, whom Ulys called Chatter, chose a thick white pine to begin the climbing adventure. The branches were so dense that climbing them was little different from working through a thicket on the ground. At least it seemed that way until Ulys neared the top of the tree and peered out. While, in truth, he was only a few feet off the ground, the vista he beheld filled him with a sense of awe and majesty. He was amazed to realize that he felt no fear—only excitement.

To a rabbit, the sensation of height was like awakening in heaven. For hours the two climbed through the small pine tree. Chatter never grew bored showing off his skill to his new friend. Only the approach of darkness caused them to part, and then with the promise to meet again in the morning.

Rachel had long grown accustomed to Ulys's sense of adventure, but this most recent tale went beyond the bounds of credibility. She listened, first in disbelief, and later in amazement and horror, as he recounted for her his adventure. Late into the night she puzzled at the wonder of this great rabbit, thrust into her simple life like a bolt of lightning from above.

What manner of creature fought with foxes and climbed trees with squirrels? None of the legends she knew so well even mentioned such behavior. What would the clan think of this new aberration? How would the new Lord react to such behavior? She knew it was no use to forbid Ulys to see the squirrel. In his quiet and gentle way, he was completely headstrong. No threat or danger seemed enough to keep him from savoring the zest of life. Once he was determined, nothing and no one could sway his course. Yet she pleaded with him to keep this newest activity a secret. Rabbits reacted to any change with skepticism and distress. Who could say how they would respond to such an incomprehensible event?

Early morning found Ulys in the apple grove, too excited even to eat. As thrilling as the pine tree had been to climb, he wanted to climb and jump in the big trees as did his friend. Chatter listened to his request. He walked around Ulys in silent thought. He noted the small ears, long legs, and sharp claws with favor. All those traits that had caused Ulys such torment in his warren existence would be to his advantage in the tree world. Silently, Chatter led him to a medium-sized, shaggy-bark hickory. Its rough surface was easy to grip. All morning long the two worked at climbing the trunk—and failed.

Ulys, with his powerful kick, could jump up into the tree for several feet and hang where he landed. The problem was the weakness of his front legs. They simply didn't afford the grip needed to stabilize him and allow climbing.

By noon, Ulys was battered and bruised, but still determined to climb. Chatter knew they needed help. He convinced Ulys to accompany him to the hickory grove and meet Chatter's family.

What a noisy scene that was! Ulys was almost deafened by all the squirrels' bantering and shouting. Never had a rabbit dared to come so far from the warren to visit the squirrels' home. Always before, if the squirrels had greeted a rabbit, it had provoked a response of terror and headlong flight. When, at Chatter's urging, Ulys climbed a small pine, the squirrels' collective response was enthusiastic beyond any rabbit's imagination.

Next Ulys showed the squirrels how he could jump into the hickory and hang, but that he fell when he attempted to climb higher. After witnessing repeated efforts and repeated failures to scale even one step above where he gripped the tree originally, the squirrels were puzzled as to how to help. They were enthused by the novelty of the rabbit in their presence (for unlike rabbits, squirrels love adventure). Since they climbed so effortlessly, almost from birth, they simply had no idea how to help Ulys learn a skill so natural to them. It was Chatter's own grandmother who provided the answer.

Years ago, one of her offspring had been born with withered front paws. The squirrels had no custom of placing a malformed kit out to be the prey of predators. Obtaining an adequate supply of food was no problem for them in the winter, as they were in hibernation for most of the season. The handicapped infant was safe in the warm tree nest, but all their clan worried about how the youngster could achieve a normal squirrel adulthood. Somehow, he would have to learn to climb.

Years before, the grandma had come up with a plan to assist this youngster. It consisted of three parts. First, during the winter months in the nest, the little squirrel worked long and hard to strengthen his back legs to compensate for the deformed front legs. This was no problem for Ulys, with his powerful back legs. No squirrel ever possessed the leg strength of Ulys. Second, the grandmother had used her own teeth, which could so effortlessly chew the husks off the hardest nut, to sharpen the claws of the little squirrel and improve his ability to grip the tree. Finally, the squirrel was taught to climb with the help and support of four other squirrels, who surrounded him. They protected him from injury, gave him confidence, and were also able to give advice on how to best proceed with the climbing as they went.

Ulys was eager to let the grandma sharpen his claws. He could see no possible ill side effects from the procedure, as both his running and digging abilities would be improved. As soon as this simple task was complete, Chatter and three of his friends surrounded Ulys as he started his climb up a small hickory.

With very little support from the squirrels, thanks to his newly sharpened claws, Ulys soon reached the tree branches. With their help, he climbed to the top of the small hickory they had chosen to begin their climb. There, shaky with both joy and fear, he clung and savored his accomplishment. What glory he felt! He, an outcast, had done something no other of his kind had ever even dared. He practiced climbing all day. He was slow and clumsy, but he was climbing.

8
the new lord

The next morning, as all the clan fed and visited in the warm spring grass, Ulys moved to the old bush that had sheltered the fox on that fateful day, and as casually as if he had done so all his life, he climbed to its top.

Rachel's pleas for secrecy were forgotten in his excitement. From his elevated perch, Ulys could not contain his look of joyful exuberance. He heard the murmur of the crowd. He looked down in triumph—only to see them staring up in horror! The face which registered the most shock of all was that of his beloved Rachel.

The guard rabbits were around the bush in a moment. Ulys climbed down and was immediately escorted back to the warren by the stern guards. Rachel hurried along just behind them. It was time to face the event she had dreaded for so long. It was time to meet the new Lord Rabbit.

The new Lord was young and strong. He was always the best at the games the rabbits loved to play and an equal to even the strongest guard in strength. He was pretty and popular. He was also vain and not just a little foolish.

He listened intently to the story of Ulys. His strange arrival among them and his first meeting with the old Lord were recounted by the scribe. The Lord already knew the story of the fox and the rescue of Megan and had been disturbed by such unrabbitlike behavior. He listened patiently as the guards explained why they had brought Ulys today. The shock and distraction caused by Ulys's climb could have led to death for some of the clan, since, for a rabbit, having so many natural enemies, even the briefest lapse in focus and concentration could mean death. Causing such a dangerous distraction, for any reason, was a very serious violation of warren law.

The Lord questioned Ulys about his strange climbing feat. He listened in shocked silence as Ulys told of Chatter and his family. He examined the altered claws with horror and revulsion. Finally the room grew quiet. The Lord said he had to think on such a serious matter, and they were all to return tomorrow for his decision.

Buck and Megan were among those few who supported Ulys and waited for him to appear from the Lord's chambers. They were somber and frightened at the thought of their friend being taken before the Lord. Ulys seemed less affected by the ordeal than were his friends. Throughout the evening, they reassured him that he had done no real harm. After all, no one had been hurt by his actions. As had Rachel, they advised him that he must surely stop this foolishness with trees, but they all felt he would not be too severely punished.

Rachel, in her fear, kept completely silent. Ulys said little, but as the long night passed, the thought of never again climbing into the sky seemed impossible for him to contemplate.

The Lord, to his credit, thought long and hard that night.

No normal rabbit liked change, and everything about this animal was disquieting, if for no other reason than being so unusual. To rabbits, rare meant bad. They lived a life filled with order and rules. Their happiness was in sameness. Being distracted often resulted in someone sending his or her death cry to the Great Rabbit. This sameness, or lack of change, challenge, and stimulation, was the creed that made their very existence possible. Such had always been their belief. Nothing different could be allowed or tolerated within the closed circle of the warren.

There was also the matter of the weird ears and legs, now further disfigured by the sharpened claws. Were these traits, so different from the rest of the clan, the mark of evil? The size of the young buck was also a matter that disturbed the Lord. He was so big and powerful as to be a threat to the strongest among them, even without the dangerously sharp claws. Ulys did compete in some of the games, defeating all the other youngsters in the warren effortlessly.

The path seemed clear. Rabbits took no risks. The safest path was always their choice. The safest path was to banish Ulys from the warren. Soon, away from the protection of the den, he would return to the Great Rabbit, and life in the warren would return to normal. Secure in his decision, the Lord slept.

9
the verdict

Rachel knew what the decision would be well before the Lord reached it himself. She spent a sleepless night planning. By early morning she was prepared to leave her lifetime home forever.

The formal decision shocked Ulys and his friends, but was greeted with joy by the great majority of rabbits in the warren. Both Buck and Megan offered to leave with them, but Rachel said no. Traveling away from the warren meant certain death. With no warren mouth to offer them protection, there was no defense against predators. Sadly the two touched noses with Megan and Buck, turned their backs to the warren, and, as outcasts, walked up the hill and away from what had been their home all of their lives.

Ulys pleaded with Rachel to remain in the safety of her lifelong home. He knew he'd find safety with Chatter and his family, but Rachel insisted on joining him. Ulys was her life, and to lose him would be a form of death she couldn't accept. Whatever fate held in store for them, they would endure together.

Chatter and his family could barely understand what had happened. Though they lived just a few yards from the rabbits in linear distance, their values were entirely different. None would ever be banished from the squirrel community. If a squirrel was caught by a predator, his final act was not a cry of death, but a vicious bite to the nose of his attacker. Squirrels loved excitement and adventure. Nothing thrilled them as much as something new. While unable to understand the reason the rabbits were forced from their homes, they were thrilled to have such unusual guests in their midst.

Ulys could have stayed safely with the squirrels in their tree nests, but it was impossible for Rachel to even attempt to climb a tree. Their first night out of the warren was spent in a shallow scrape they dug together, both of them cold and frightened, as their squirrel friends stood guard over them in the sheltering trees. The moaning of the spring winds and the sting of a steady rain seemed like the weeping of a god over their sad fate.

The morning dawned clear. They had survived the first night safely, but both rabbits knew that without a permanent den to flee to, at least Rachel, unable to climb from danger, was doomed. Both fed quietly on the lush grass under the squirrels' homes and brooded silently on this disturbing thought.

Rachel had spent her whole life with a rabbit's calm acceptance of death. But seeing and listening to Ulys had made her reflect. She was no longer willing to go quietly to the beyond. She had come to believe, like her adopted son, that there was more to life than simple acceptance of whatever fate offered.

Suddenly the quiet morning feed was interrupted by what seemed to Rachel the sounds of fury itself. In reality, it was only the excited chatter of a few of the squirrels, but to one raised in the relative quiet of the warren, it seemed an explosion of noise.

The great commotion was merely a greeting for two very timid rabbits. A shy doe and a big buck approached Rachel and Ulys. They were Megan and Buck, determined to cast their fate with their two friends. After a long, sleepless night, they too had decided they could no longer accept the rules and laws of the warren. They had quietly slipped off before dawn to join their friends.

The squirrels all looked down from their trees, greatly moved by the sight of the four rabbits, knowing they faced almost certain death, quietly touching noses and pledging eternal friendship in the sunlit glade.

10
megan and buck

Ulys had not allowed Rachel and his friends to accompany him into the world outside the den just to perish. He knew they all faced great danger. Even Ulys, with his unique ability to climb, his powerful kick, and his unusual rabbit strength, was no match for a larger predator such as a wolf or an eagle. They had to find permanent shelter, and find it soon, or surely they would all join the Great Rabbit.

It was possible they could search and find another warren. They knew that other rabbit clans did exist. But rabbits hate change, and there was a good chance they would be driven off by a new clan to again face their destiny alone. Ulys had little inclination to place his fate once again in the hands of others.

Ulys had suspected for a while that the day of his exile

might come. He knew that Rachel would not leave him, and while comforted by this knowledge, he knew that with Rachel along, finding safety would be much harder. He had tried, in a most unrabbitlike manner, to create a plan for their safety. But a new warren was hard to dig, even for an entire clan. It was an impossible task for four rabbits to undertake. Also, to create a new home, they would have to find a location with water nearby and sheltered from the weather. Even if it was possible for them to dig their own warren, where would they do so? It seemed hopeless.

Never one to give up or remain discouraged for long, Ulys spent the day climbing with Chatter. He no longer needed the aid of others to climb the easier trees. As they moved freely through the bowers (to the utter amazement of both rabbits and squirrels who looked on), the two friends discussed the problem facing the rabbits. As Chatter began to fully understand the danger of their plight, he grew more and more upset. The idea of these brave and daring friends becoming food for the many predators that hunted them was unthinkable to him.

Maybe it was due to their elevation, or maybe the seriousness of their plight heightened their awareness. No one reason can be established for certain, but legend has it that at this exact moment, the Great Rabbit chose to intervene. Whatever the cause, Ulys's eye was suddenly drawn to the sun striking what seemed to be a cloud far away, atop the mountain. He stared long and hard at the twisting stream of mist wafting gently upward in the breeze of the warming day. Finally he asked Chatter what the wavering column was.

Chatter explained that what they were looking at was a common sight for the squirrels to observe on days when the temperature warmed. What caused the strange land-bound cloud no squirrel had ever tried to discover. After a second of thought, Ulys asked Chatter if he would dare the journey to discover the cause of such an unusual phenomenon with him. Ulys had no idea what he would find, but he sensed that it was something he was fated to explore.

Chatter hesitated not a minute. Though the mountain was the home of eagles and wolves alike, he understood his friend's urgency. The trip would require two days, and none but the two young adventurers would go. They could spend their night in the safety of a tree. Though the area from which the vapor rose was high on the mountain above the tree line (and thus, with their best chance of a climbing escape not existent, an area of great danger to them both), they jumped from the tree they were in, eager to tell their friends of their plans.

The three other rabbits were not in favor of the journey. They understood that if Ulys were lost, it would mean the end for them all. But, the intensity in the eyes of Ulys finally stilled their questions and they reluctantly agreed. The squirrels promised to protect the three while their friends were gone and even set out to help them dig a deeper temporary den under the roots of a fragrant bush, where their scent would be difficult for enemies to detect. If they stayed in their den those few days, they would be safe.

Their friends' safety assured, Chatter and Ulys wasted no time in beginning their journey. To the waves and cheers of rabbits and squirrels alike, they headed up the mountain.

11
the journey

The day turned warm and lovely. As long as they traveled in the forest, they had little to fear. Ulys's hearing and vision would warn them of danger much earlier than Chatter would have normally sensed it. Their ability to climb all but insured their safety if they remained vigilant. The hike was difficult, but not dangerous. As they rose in elevation, both noticed plants not seen on the lowlands. They grazed on the tender and unusual young delicacies as they progressed up the hill. This change in their diet, after a lifetime of lowland foods, was a treat. The beauty of the day, the unusual and delicious food, and the thrill of new adventure gave a pleasant tone to the journey.

Ulys noted with satisfaction the appearance of several

small streams coming off the mountain. He had no clear concept of what he hoped to accomplish on this journey, just a feeling of the need to make it, but he was constantly on the lookout for anything that could be of help to him and his friends. A site for a new warren was their first and most critical need. Maybe, with the right location and the help of the squirrels, they could create their own home and safety.

As the pair worked their way slowly but steadily toward the still-visible tower of mist, both listened and smelled for signs of danger. None appeared, and the day proceeded pleasantly apace. As the sky began to darken, the two friends looked for and found shelter in a large hollow tree, easily climbed by Ulys. In it they passed a peaceful and restful night; both were worn out by the long journey and yet stimulated by their adventure. It seemed with each passing moment their bond of friendship grew. Chatter was as determined as Ulys to find a safe home for his new friends.

They were up at first light and on their way. Both realized they had to find the source of the mist and return at least to the tree line by nightfall. A night spent on the rocky, bare mountain face was too dangerous to contemplate.

Yet the mist seemed to recede as they journeyed. They soon left the cover of the woods behind and moved to the treacherous open mountain face. In the totally unfamiliar terrain, Ulys wished Rachel and her wisdom had accompanied them, but he knew that was impossible. All they could do was push on quickly and attempt to solve the mystery of the strange cloud they seemed destined to seek.

At last they arrived at a cliff edge from which the cloud source could be seen. The mist seemed to come from the solid rock itself. As they cautiously approached, they saw a small stream of water running out directly below the misty vapor. Ulys approached carefully and sniffed. Gently he touched the water and mist. He pulled back his paw quickly. They both felt hot to the touch!

The opening from which the stream and mist escaped

allowed no chance of entry, even for the svelte Chatter. Both sensed that some great mystery lay behind this mouth. Ulys was more experienced underground. If there were something there, possibly some type of chamber, they would have to search elsewhere for an entrance. Ulys searched up the mountain from the hot stream, and Chatter down from the mouth. In just a few minutes Ulys discovered it.

The opening he sought was revealed by accident, or so says the legend. His sharpened claws dislodged a rock and started a slide. Ulys went tumbling down the slope with the sliding rock, crying frantically for Chatter to get clear. At last he was able to stop his fall on a flat outcrop. When the worried Chatter arrived to help him, they both stared up the mountain face to where the slide had started. A small hole now appeared in the mountain wall. From this new opening the faintest of mists wafted up into the cool mountain air.

Both animals felt very uncomfortable and exposed on the bare rock wall, so devoid of the vital shelter they needed for survival. They quickly ascended the short distance and, without the slightest hesitation, stepped inside the opening.

What they saw took their breath away. It was a large chamber, filled with an eerie light. As their eyes adjusted to the dimness of the interior, they could see fissures, or cracks, on the sides of the cavern that allowed a slight amount of light to penetrate the large subterranean space.

Through the bottom of the cavern ran the little stream, no longer emitting steam inside the mountain. As they hopped down to the floor of the cavern and the shallow stream, they could see grasses and moss growing on the rocks and soils of the stream's edge. A few nibbles proved these tender morsels to be delicious.

12
the cave

The two friends sat quietly, in awe of what their senses revealed. The smells of fresh growth and fragrant water in the cavern were delightful. The sounds, too, were extraordinary. There was utter silence, except for the musical tinkle of the tiny stream wandering through the enclosure. The air was pleasantly warm and had a rich texture. As their eyes adjusted more and more to the light, they could see that the space they had entered was huge.

Both friends silently assessed what they had discovered. They realized this was the perfect habitat for some animals. The pleasant temperature meant that squirrels could avoid hibernation in winter and still come to no harm from the elements. A continuous supply of water, and at least some food, was available without the animals being forced to venture outside and risk the danger such exposure brought.

True, the lack of trees meant no nuts, no safe and sheltering hollow tree or limbs to hide and play in, and thus the mountainside could never be a true home to squirrels. Indeed, what squirrel could stand to live underground? Even the brief underground journey so far was unnerving to Chatter, and none among the squirrels could equal his courage. Yet, as a place for squirrels to visit and spend time in the winter, it was ideal.

It took Ulys only a moment to realize that this cave might be the answer to his prayers. To create a warren from this natural underearth space, no digging would be required, except to create individual dens in the edges of the huge cavern. That could be accomplished easily and at their leisure. All their problems seemed answered by this place, except one. That crucial question was safety.

Ulys had smelled the rich air, fragrant with the scent of living plants and the abundant moisture. His nose was more sensitive than Chatter's, however, and he smelled one more thing. In the air of the cave there existed a faint but definite presence. Some living creature had been or was within this space, and its exact nature had to be discovered before they could guarantee a safe home for their friends.

It took just a few moments for the two explorers to find an enclave through which a stream flowed. From the stream rose the fateful mist which had drawn the animals there. They decided to journey back through the large cavern and together explore its confines. They spent the rest of the morning engaged in that task and finally found what Ulys knew had to exist—a separate passage into the cavern.

The mouth to this second opening was small. None of the faint light from the cavern's fissured walls penetrated back to expose its existence. The two adventurers decided to feed and drink in the cavern and discuss how best to proceed.

Chatter didn't want to enter that small space. He'd had his

fill of the underground and suggested they simply cover over the opening and return to their friends. Ulys would have liked to agree, but his keener sense of smell had confirmed for him what his sixth sense had warned him of. The presence lurked within that dark, narrow passage. Its scent was unfamiliar but sinister. Once again he wished Rachel and her great wisdom were with them. But all along he knew—that passage was a place he had to enter.

Chatter tried to talk him out of it. The dark, twisted passageway left no room for escape in case of sudden danger. Ulys argued that he must go. He could leave no possible threat unexplored if he planned to return with his friends. He encouraged Chatter to remain in the cavern and wait for his return. As badly as Chatter wished to accept that advice, he couldn't leave his friend. Together, with Ulys in the lead, they entered the darkness and mystery of the passage.

At first, they could see nothing and groped blindly down the narrow tunnel. Often the way became so tiny they were forced to crawl. The way was as constricted and dark as the exit from the womb. Finally the passage opened and travel became quicker. Also, either their vision had adjusted or there was some source of light, as now they could see—not well, but they could see.

Despite all their care and their keen senses, when danger threatened, it took them by complete surprise. Perhaps they grew careless with fatigue. Maybe the strange atmosphere of the passage dulled or confused their senses. Maybe what happened was simply their fate.

They had turned to explore a small side passage of the cave. Ulys was determined to leave nothing to chance, but to explore every conceivable source of danger. The side passage was a dead end. Ulys's senses were more acute, so he led the two through the cavern. As they returned through the main passage, Ulys began to think that perhaps the danger he had sensed was only the natural odor of such a rocky passage. He was considering returning to the cavern when his bent ears heard a slight sound of movement. He froze instantly and was bumped into by Chatter. His protests were quickly stopped by the sound of a hiss. The sound froze them both and almost made them faint. Though neither had ever seen that which now faced them, they both instantly knew its name. It was a rattlesnake, and it held them captive in the dead-end passage they had entered.

Ulys quickly realized the trap. The snake had sensed them long before they were aware of his presence. He had led them to this place, as they followed his slight spore, and deliberately chosen just the right place to block them in. He had done his work well. They were trapped in the tiny dead-end passage, with no hope of escape.

The rattler swelled until his bulk almost filled the tiny passageway. He was in no hurry to deal with them, as he knew full well the hopelessness of their situation. He swayed slightly and announced to the terrified pair, "My name is Xan. Welcome to my home. I get so few visitors anymore that indeed this is a singular pleasure."

Chatter almost collapsed in terror, but Ulys began to study the reptile intently. It seemed the snake was to give them some time, if only for his own amusement. Ulys was determined to use this gift of time, even if the few moments granted were to be his last. Not only Ulys's life was in the balance, but the life of Chatter—and his rabbit companions, waiting trustingly for him in the hickory grove, were in danger as well.

As he studied the snake, he saw that indeed it was huge. He never dreamed a reptile so large existed! But slowly he realized that it was also very old. He felt some relief in the knowledge that he possessed two weapons—time and the advantage of youth. Maybe there was hope in this hopeless situation.

"We welcome you, Xan, and apologize for our intrusion. We had no idea that this was your home. We will leave you now in peace," said Ulys.

"Your apology is well put and accepted, my new friends;

however, leaving here is a thing you will never do. The gods were kind to deliver you to me, as I am weak from hunger. I was just about to leave the cavern in search of food when I sensed your entrance. I have waited patiently and long for such a gift, as I would rather face the enemy of hunger than the claws of the eagle."

"We would be honored to bring you some food, noble and powerful Xan. We know of a nest of young mice near the cavern. If you could excuse us a moment, we'll return with them," said Ulys.

"You are too kind; but I fear my hunger is too acute for me to accept your gracious offer. I do have an offer for you in return. I will now strike and devour one of you. I am sad to say the process can be unpleasant. I would suggest that one of you retreat to the back of the passage and thus avoid the distressing sight. I would further suggest the other step bravely forward. I will strike quickly and your spirit will flee without discomfort."

Ulys replied, "We seem at your mercy. May we retire back down the passage for a moment and make our choice, great snake?"

"Yes, but make haste, or I will follow and deal with you there," hissed the great monster.

Ulys and Chatter fled to the back of the passage. Ulys spoke quickly and told Chatter that he had a plan. Chatter would have to be courageous and wait for his action. No time could be spent in explanation. Ulys touched Chatter's nose, told him to be still and listen, and turned to approach Xan.

"I compliment both your courage and your wisdom," spoke Xan, as he saw Ulys approaching.

"I fear none but the Great Rabbit, whom I am soon to meet," said Ulys.

As he spoke, Ulys slowly advanced toward the great snake. He held his forepaws behind him, thrust forth his breast, and lifted his head to bare his chest.

Xan swelled even larger. As the brave rabbit approached,

he thought how rabbitlike this one was to so easily accept his doom. He was unable to coil in the tight passage, so he had to let the rabbit come very close before his strike. With Xan's advanced years, no movements were fast or easy. At last the range was right and the rabbit's vulnerable breast was exposed. With no hesitation, thought of compassion, or warning, Xan struck.

Poor Chatter waited in terror. How had a tree dweller come to this, trapped in an underground tomb and at the mercy of a giant reptile? Snakes were hardly a danger to a squirrel. None lived in the trees of their forest. Chatter was so undone by it all, he hadn't even protested when Ulys decided to go back alone to face the snake. Now, with a few moments to compose himself, he was ashamed of his cowardly behavior. Surely he and Ulys could fight. Even if somehow they slew the great snake, they would be trapped in the passage and die slowly. But, to accept death without a struggle was not the way of his kind. He took a deep breath and started quickly back through the passageway after his friend.

The sound that stopped him was like no other he had ever heard. It was a sound of terror, pain, and rage. It was the sound of a snake.

Chatter abandoned his fear. He raced to Ulys's side. There he found his friend standing calmly in the passage. Before him the great snake writhed, obviously in agony. The sight of the loathsome creature unnerved Chatter anew, but despite his fears, he raced to join Ulys.

His friend turned and, with a grin, held up an object for Chatter to see. As he approached, the frightened squirrel could make out a flat, thin sliver of rock, held firmly in Ulys's sharp claws. Looking at the rabbit's feet, he saw the two terrible fangs of the great beast lying on the passage floor in a pool of reptilian blood.

Ulys had noticed the thin sliver of stone when they first explored the passage. He had developed his desperate idea as they had proceeded together toward the back of the dead-end cavern. On his return to where Xan lay in wait, he had gathered the shard of flint and held it behind him. The snake had struck a death blow with all his might in the tiny passage. Ulys had been quicker, flashing the flint shield in front of the obvious target of the reptile's venom. Now the snake lay completely helpless before them. Once again a combination of speed, daring, and courage, plus the attitude, so unrabbitlike, of confronting one's challenges, had served the young heroes well. The friends rejoiced.

But, soon they realized that while they had rendered the snake completely harmless, he still blocked their passage to freedom. Xan had recovered enough to be still. He glared at the two, in both fear and hatred. Ulys regarded him a moment, then went right up to the beast. He placed a paw on the snake's nose and said calmly, "Xan, my friend, it is now you who needs us. We will help you. Follow us to the chamber and we can get moss and mud to stop your pain and bleeding. Together we will plan a way for you to feed."

The old snake glared at them. "You have killed me," he said. "Why should I believe a word you say?"

"You have little choice," said Ulys. "And we have need of you. Let us return to the chamber and ease your pain."

Slowly the old snake backed from the passage. The two friends moved past him and retraced their way to the chamber. They packed the evulsed fang sockets with moss and mud. The bleeding and pain decreased and at last the weakened old reptile slept.

13
life with xan

Chatter wanted to flee while the snake slept. His mind knew the old, defanged snake no longer was a danger to them, but his emotions couldn't ignore the fear and dread the giant creature inspired.

As Ulys had been returning to the main cavern with the creature, he had devised a plan. He knew he needed Xan for his knowledge of the cavern and for his protection from other mountain predators, whom the lowland rabbits weren't as yet familiar with. This cavern seemed the only hope for his clan, yet its differences from a normal den would concern the other rabbits. Despite all the advantages the cave presented for them—shelter, food, water, and warmth—their natural fear of the unknown would tend to drive them away. Had not the discovery of Xan proved those fears justified?

Yet, with Xan and his knowledge of the cave, they could live in relative safety. His keen viper senses could detect the slightest danger underground. His mere presence would terrify any possible intruder. But a snake with no fangs, even if it weren't old, weak, and in pain, would soon be a dead snake. Such was the Creator's will. Ulys struggled desperately to devise a plan to rescue the reptile whose fangs had shattered against the stone.

Suddenly he remembered the flint. From the same area of the passage where he had picked up the thin sheet of stone that had so effectively defanged his vastly superior opponent, Ulys recalled long, sharp fragments that had also littered the floor. Ulys crept quietly away as Chatter slept and hurried back to the passage. The huge and deadly fangs still lay in pieces on the ground in a pool of reptile blood. Ulys found two shards of flint of the exact shape and size of the ruined fangs. He seized them quickly and hurried back to the cavern.

Xan was awake. Wasting no time, Ulys pressed him with his plan. The shards would be inserted into the fangs' sockets. He would have no venom, of course, but the fangs were needed only to hold the prey, which the snake then would swallow whole.

Ulys explained that they had seen mice dens on the mountainside. The rabbits and squirrels were no friends of mice, since they ate the same foods. In the dying months of winter, often the presence of mice in the warren area meant death to the very old and the very young among the rabbits. Possibly they could work together to eliminate the mice that threatened the rabbits' food supply and at the same time feed Xan.

In return they would require the help of Xan in patrolling the cavern and ensuring their safety from intruders. The mere presence of the great reptile would drive away all but the most fierce of beasts with no more effort than a casual rattle of his imposing tale.

Xan had little choice but to agree. Carefully the moss and

mud were removed from the no-longer-bleeding sockets. Ulys gently fitted the flints into place, and Chatter, with his amazingly sharp teeth, trimmed and shaped them to fit. In a short while, the crude replacements had been inserted. Night was falling, and despite the trauma of the day, the strange trio all slept.

Ulys was up before full light. He knew the unexplained absence of the adventurers for a second night would have both the rabbits and squirrels deeply concerned. He fully understood and accepted the fact that Rachel, Megan, and Buck were completely dependent on him for any hope of their survival. He and Chatter had to find a way to feed Xan and return quickly to their friends.

But the plan of capturing mice that had seemed so possible in theory the night before seemed much more difficult in the light of day. Not only do rabbits not kill, but in his young life Ulys had already developed a hatred for meaningless death. Death seemed representative of all the things he could not accept in the code of the warren.

Suddenly he leapt to his feet, both waking and startling his companions. Chatter had no sooner calmed down from this rude interruption of his needed rest when he turned to see the coiled Xan and was shocked again.

Ignoring the drowsiness and weakness of the snake and the agitation of Chatter, Ulys began to expound on his sudden inspiration.

"If not mice, then why not what mice eat?" spoke Ulys.

"What in the world are you babbling about?" asked Chatter.

Ulys hurried to explain his plan. The old snake was fading quickly from hunger and the shock of the previous day's ordeal. The two friends wasted no time explaining the plan to the faint reptile, but instead hurried to accomplish their goal.

The theory was simple enough—rather than feed Xan the mice he preferred, they would feed him instead the things the mice ate. These seeds and grasses were easy to find and were quickly gathered. Ulys and Chatter chewed them to a fine mash and Ulys delicately forced the bolus down the weakened reptile's throat. The two friends then drank and fed themselves. By the time they had eaten, Xan had visibly revived.

They explained to the now-conscious reptile what they had done to bring him back from the doors of his Creator. Xan disliked the idea of eating plant matter, but his mouth was so sore and his new stone fangs so grotesque that he couldn't complain much. The two friends gathered and prepared further sustenance for the great reptile and explained their plan to return to him, along with their friends, in two days. They asked him to guard the cave and keep it safe and promised to gather an assortment of foods on the journey as a reward for his efforts. Xan reluctantly agreed.

For the ancient reptile to be reduced to working with (if not indeed for) those who all his life had been considered nothing but his dinner was, to say the least, a revolting development. But weakness from hunger, loss of blood, and age, to say nothing of sporting rocks where his beloved fangs had been, removed most of his objections. Better to work with rodents and eat plants than die slowly of starvation. It seemed his fate was truly sealed.

As the two comrades left the cave and hurried for the trees below, they agreed that they would both feel better if their new, large cavemate became a strict vegetarian.

14
the new home

    Once they reached the shelter of the trees, the trip down the mountain proved quick and uneventful. The only scare on the whole journey occurred when a large shadow passed over them, just on the edge of the tree line. The scream of an eagle that followed sent Ulys and Chatter bolting to the nearest tree. Ulys climbed its protecting limbs with an agility he had no idea he possessed.
    Though they survived that first encounter with the king of the airways, Ulys realized that on the mountain, eagles would pose a great threat to their safety. Some solution to this problem would have to be found. Return to the Great Rabbit was quick and sure once rabbits were seized by the fierce talons of these ferocious raptors.

When Chatter and Ulys returned to their friends in the hickory grove, they were greeted with great joy. Indeed, all had feared for their safety. As rabbit and squirrel alike gathered around the great tree to hear of their adventure, none could give complete credence to the tale they were told. When all of the questions had been asked and finally answered, both squirrels and rabbits looked at the two travelers with a mixture of awe and disbelief.

Rachel thought long and hard through the night about the incredible story she had been told. The adventures on the epic journey terrified her, yet she knew that they all were tempting fate, living in their shallow dig, even with the protection and cooperation of their new squirrel friends. By morning it was agreed. They had no choice but to undertake a desperate journey to this strange new warren and confront this terrifying creature with the stone fangs.

Chatter and two of his young cousins agreed to accompany the rabbits on this journey. The trip was many times more dangerous with this large group, and increasingly so due to the fact that three of the rabbits couldn't climb to avoid danger. Chatter's two cousins were young adults and ready for great adventure. The party received the send-off of heroes as they embarked on their dangerous journey.

Rachel, once committed to the trip, went about the journey in a businesslike manner. She moved slowly and carefully through the strange forest, always on the alert for danger, observing all as she passed. The three squirrels stuck to the treetops for greater safety and also to enable them to detect and give early warning of any danger.

There was great joy among the younger rabbits. All had realized when they left the warren that they might soon face the Great Rabbit. Buck and Megan had accepted this as their fate, as the rabbits of the warren were wont to do. Ulys had never for one instant given in to such thinking. More than that, he had willingly accepted the burden of the safety of the others as his responsibility. Of the four, he was the most relieved at finding them a place of safety in which to dwell.

Rachel remained quiet, deep in thought. Certainly she felt no desire to join in the gaiety of the three youngsters, but she could think of no other course open to them except the one they were embarking upon; yet even the short journey up the mountain filled her with dread. To remain even a few feet from the safety of a mouth was an unnatural and terrifying action to the old doe.

A choice was made to spend the night in the forest, not far from the edge of the tree line. Again they all labored together to dig a scrape under a fragrant bush, near a small stream. All had to admit that the food they were finding on the journey was a welcome relief and change. Some of the new growth was unknown even to Rachel, but delicious to them all.

As night approached, the squirrels spread out around the scrape, in the safety of the treetops. Ulys, despite Rachel's objections, settled down in the scrape with his friends, disdaining the greater safety of the surrounding oaks.

It was near morning when disaster struck. The eastern sky was lightening with the first rays of dawn. All of the company, despite their fears, were sleeping deeply, exhausted by the work and worry of the unusual journey.

The first warning was sounded by one of the squirrels in the trees. The frantic cry soon sounded throughout the encampment—wolf!

On land, a wolf was by far the most dangerous of the many predators that fed on the rabbit. In size, speed, strength, and cunning, none matched this gray ghost of the forest. True to the nature of his kind, he had smelled the rabbits, despite the cloaking aroma of the shrubbery they had tunneled under. He had silently worked his way downwind of the clan and approached from that direction.

Two things saved the rabbits from a sad end. A blue jay, perched in a tree above the wolf's path of approach, had called out a warning. This had immediately alerted the squirrel, who had roused the camp. The other factor that protected them was the result of their own careful planning. Since the scrape was under a flowering bush, the wolf could smell rabbits, but not locate them exactly. His frustration at not knowing precisely where his prey was hidden had slowed him down and prevented a direct charge of the tiny dig, which would have been fatal for the four huddled there together.

Chatter and Ulys had planned for such an encounter. At once the three squirrels ran to the trees nearest the wolf and raised a tremendous racket. The wolf was angered and distracted. He jumped for the visible squirrels as they moved off through the trees, with their attacker in furious pursuit.

As soon as they were out of sight, Ulys led his small group on a frantic break over the treeless mountainside. They didn't stop until they reached and entered the protection of the cavern.

Rabbits are used to dashes, for fun, sport, and safety. But no rabbit can run hard for long. By the time they reached the cave, all were exhausted. Rachel was so worn out she could barely hop. Only the terror caused by the presence of their ancient enemy, the wolf, with no sheltering den mouth nearby, had kept them moving to the safety of this strange mountain mouth.

Ulys led Rachel and the rest down to the stream. They drank deeply of the warm water and slowly revived. They had just begun to tentatively nibble on the tender vegetation that grew along the stream's course when they heard the warning rattle of the large snake.

As they all leapt in terror to flee, they were amazed at Ulys. He leaped too, but toward the snake, and with real anger. He knew the rabbits were exhausted, and Xan's antics had further weakened them.

But Xan had simply sensed a presence and reacted as a snake in a weakened condition is wont to do. Ulys calmed down and realized that this very reaction would add to the safety of the den. He had no luck in convincing the others that Xan's reactions were germane to their best interests. They were so terrified of the huge reptile that Ulys finally had to banish Xan to the narrow passage where their first meeting had taken place.

Two problems remained. In the frantic fleeing from the wolf, no food for Xan had been harvested. Xan was much recovered after his rest and feeding, but was hungry again. Even brave Ulys didn't relish the thought of sharing space with a hungry rattler.

Of equal concern was the well-being of Chatter and his friends. Ulys knew they were much faster over long runs than the rabbits and was worried that they hadn't reached the cavern yet.

He decided to leave the others and collect food for the seemingly insatiable appetite of Xan, while searching for the squirrels at the same time. Cautioning the others not to leave the cavern under any circumstances, he crept carefully to the mouth.

As he peered cautiously out, searching for wolf or eagle, he saw the squirrels approaching. But, they were going slowly, and there were only two. Ulys rushed out to meet them.

15
the hand of death

Chatter was in a sad state. As soon as he had been helped to the cavern and refreshed himself with a drink and a bite of tender moss, he and his friend began to recount the ordeal that they had endured since they parted company with the rabbits just a few short moments before.

As had been the plan, the squirrels, from the relative safety of the trees, had drawn the wolf away from the rabbits. All had gone well until the wolf had heard or sensed the rabbits fleeing from their hiding place. The large beast had been enraged by the flight of his original prey and quickly changed directions, racing after the vulnerable rabbits. The squirrels, from the vantage point of the treetops, soon realized the wolf would easily catch their friends well before they could reach the longed-for safety of the mouth.

Once Chatter had reached this conclusion, he had done a foolish but daring thing. He had left the safety of the trees and leaped to the ground directly behind the hard-charging wolf. This ploy had worked, as the wolf was momentarily distracted by the unexpected appearance of the squirrel on the ground so near him, and had hesitated for a moment, indecisive over which prey to pursue. He finally chose to chase the much closer squirrel and abandon his pursuit of the rabbits.

Chatter had been careful in his daring leap to the ground to stay near a tree. Now he waited until the wolf was very close to him, before nimbly jumping back to the safety of the bowers. He avoided the wolf's frantic grab by mere inches and reached the safety of the nearby tree. However, one of his cousins, fearing for Chatter's life, had also jumped to the ground in an attempt to draw the wolf's deadly charge from Chatter. Sadly, this strategy worked only too well, as the wolf veered suddenly from his pursuit of Chatter, and the young squirrel was snapped up in his terrible jaws in seconds.

The horrified squirrels had pursued the wolf, screaming at him, but of course to no avail. The wolf reached his den, and the two despondent comrades returned to the cavern and their friends.

A deep gloom descended on the six survivors. All felt somewhat to blame for the tragedy—none more so than Chatter. In risking his life for his friends' safety, he had never stopped to consider the possible acts of his young companions. As the leader and oldest member of the trio, he felt the death of his cousin to be his fault.

Ulys and his friends felt great remorse too, as this brave youngster had died to save them. Yet, even Ulys, who questioned the rabbit beliefs more than any other, took solace in knowing the young squirrel had returned to his gods. That concept Ulys had never challenged. His disagreement with the philosophy and legends of the clan was with their ready acceptance of this return.

Chatter and his friend, however, were inconsolable. Part of the fierceness of the squirrels' nature (both took some solace in the fact that their doomed friend had given the wolf's nose a nasty bite that left him screaming in anger and pain) was in their belief in the importance of his life. No squirrel, under any conditions or circumstances, would ever be put out on the forest edge to return to the Creator. Chatter's grandmother's story of the deformed kit illustrated that. While such a creed gave them great zest and strength in life, it left them desolated by grief and loss.

In the restless night that followed, Ulys thought of this difference in beliefs between rabbit and squirrel and how it affected so deeply the patterns of the lives of those involved. Already, Ulys saw himself as a leader, even if he had accepted the position reluctantly. As the leader of this small group of docile creatures, his ideas and beliefs would deeply influence how their lives would be lived.

The fact that they now had shelter, even if it was somewhat unconventional by rabbit standards, and guarded by a huge reptile, was of great relief to Ulys. But he knew a clan of four could not survive. Each member of the tiny clan was too precious to the integrity of the group to even consider the loss of one.

It was during this night of grief and mourning that Ulys's philosophy crystallized. He refused to abandon his ideas of the Great Rabbit. In many ways they were what defined the rabbit as a species. Yet, to this he must add his fierce philosophy of the sacredness of life and the obligation of all rabbits to maintain their existence by any way possible. He felt this belief was consistent with the Great Rabbit's legend. Surely he had not given in to his many jealous rivals, so why should his earthly counterparts so easily accept what they chose to call fate?

His mental confusion resolved, Ulys finally slept, still filled with sorrow, but more at peace within his own mind. His last thought was that as soon as he could, he would find a way to add new members to their tiny clan.

16
morning on the mountain

The morning came to each of the strange band in the cavern in a different fashion.

The two squirrels awoke after a fitful night. Chatter was still deeply disturbed by the fate of his cousin. He knew his duty, which was to return at once to the hickory trees and inform all of his clan of their loss. This sad task had to be done at once.

Yet, while he had no fear of the journey itself, knowing he and his cousin would be safe once in the forest, he was deeply saddened to leave the rabbits. He would miss his strange but marvelous new friend Ulys. His daring and force of character had already deeply affected Chatter's very existence.

Also, he knew that the situation of the rabbits, in this

strange new environment, was still precarious. They were in great danger and needed all the help they could get.

Despite these concerns, Chatter's duty to his clan was clear and paramount. He roused his cousin and bid him prepare to leave while he went to talk with Ulys.

Xan, too, had awakened. The scents of the animals in the cavern were maddening to him. He was also very hungry. Little thought had been given to him in the turmoil of the last days. He wasn't strong enough yet to be able to feed himself, even on a diet of mice. He had no idea how his makeshift fangs would function with even the smallest of live prey. He was unable to eat or digest the plants and seeds the rabbits found for him unless they were chewed for him. He hated what had happened to him and the dependence it had forced upon him. But the strength of a reptile lies in its singleness of purpose. That purpose now for Xan was simple indeed. He needed food, so he set out to find Ulys.

Rachel had slept little that long night. Her older body ached from the rigors of travel, and her mind reeled from the events of the last few days. She, in typical rabbit fashion, accepted the loss of the squirrel with equanimity. She was grateful to all the squirrels for their support and succor, but when the Creator called, who could question?

What had kept her awake throughout the long night was her attempt to deal with the drastic changes that were occurring with such disturbing rapidity in their lives. Rachel had experienced more change in the last few days than she had previously experienced in her lifetime, and she didn't like it one bit. What rabbit would?

When she left the warren to be with Ulys, she had known she faced great danger, even possible death. She had accepted these things with grace. Now her mind whirled. How could it be that in a few short days she had left behind her entire life, had journeyed up the mountain in the company of squirrels to live in a cave guarded by a great snake? It made her dizzy to think of it all. Slowly, she stirred her aching body. She needed to talk with Ulys.

Megan and Buck awoke refreshed and a little thrilled at their adventure. Maybe it was this trait in their natures that had given the siblings the courage to follow Rachel and Ulys from their home. They, too, were sad at what fate had befallen the squirrel, but accepted it. What surprised—no, amazed—the two youngsters was that they were having a ball. In their brief lives in the warren, they had accepted the safety and routine. It was indeed all they had ever known. Now every minute seemed an adventure. They wanted to hurry and find Ulys, to see what new excitement this day would bring.

Ulys awoke refreshed. He had slept well, once his mind had become comfortable with their fate, and he had become clearer in his own personal philosophy.

Chatter reached Ulys first. Ulys understood and respected the squirrels' duty to return at once with their sad tidings. The two squirrels promised to come back to the mountain as soon as they could. Without eating, they set out on their journey home. In their grief, they had no wish to see the others before leaving but gently touched noses with Ulys and quietly left the cavern. Ulys followed them to the mouth and watched until he could see them safely into the trees.

As he returned to feed and drink in the cavern, Ulys saw Xan making his painful way from the passage. Suddenly he remembered they had forgotten to feed him in the sorrow and confusion of the day before. He needed the help of this creature to protect that which he had already come to see as their new home. He had to feed him at once.

As he turned to go for food, the other three rabbits approached. Without a sound or message being given, they all touched noses on the cavern floor. The four had chosen, for good or bad, to be together. Great dangers they had already faced, and surely would face again. Each had proven his or her strength and value to the others, as well as their love. The silent ceremony was their pledge of fidelity, given to each other on this beginning morn of their new lives together.

Ulys was first to speak. His plan was that they should go

as a group to explore the mountain and bring food back for themselves and Xan. He explained exactly how the reptile must be fed, and that only he would do the actual feeding (to the others' great relief). They all had to help in gathering food for the giant snake. They needed to locate a large source of the seeds and grasses the mice ate to feed the hungry Xan.

They emerged slowly from the mouth together. The strange, rocky, windy, and treeless land intimidated them. As they moved cautiously from the mouth, Ulys warned them of the great raptors that lived on the mountain's crest. He told them to be continually on the lookout for hiding places among the rocks. While not as plentiful a place for safety as the bushes and plants below, once among the rocks they were physically out of the reach of the large mountain predators.

Feeding themselves and finding food for Xan was easy. In the springtime, every small dent in the soil was alive with new plant growth. The rocky soil held water and thus plants were both plentiful and tender. They had fed themselves and were gathering Xan's food to take back when a large shadow passed slowly over them. They all bolted in terror for the mouth.

From the safety of the cave, Ulys peered up to discover the cause of their fright. It was simply an old crow, now laughing raucously at the timid rabbits' flight. Ulys was upset at the thought of their mindless panic. The four agreed that they must take turns as guard rabbits, paying special attention to the skies in their new home. Only three would be free to feed and gather for the four rabbits and Xan, but right now food was so plentiful that that was not a reason for concern. Ulys thought again of their small numbers and worried. What if one of them were to become lost?

Quickly, Xan's food was regathered. Ulys showed them how to prepare it and, to the horror of the others, quickly and efficiently fed Xan. The sight of the rock fangs terrified the others into a state of near paralysis. Xan, once fed, retreated down the passage to sleep and to heal.

Ulys cautioned Rachel and Megan to remain in the cave

for the rest of the day and to explore their new home closely. He and Buck were going to search the area around the mouth. The four touched noses, and the two bucks left.

Rachel and Megan did explore. They agreed to no longer feed on the tender moss inside the cave, tempting and delicious as it was. Rachel had lived through many a dying season. In her wisdom, she knew that, on the harsh mountainside, this food resource would be essential to their survival during the long winter months to come.

The two friends carefully explored the cavern walls to find the perfect spots to dig their dens. For comfort, warmth, and security, they would dig two dens, one for Ulys and Rachel, the other for Buck and Megan. In the tradition of rabbits, Rachel, in her mind, planned for a whole series of dens leading out from the cave walls. True, they had but one doe that was capable of bearing a litter, but to plan for clan expansion honored the way of the Great Rabbit. When all was planned in their minds, the two began to dig their cozy dens in the hard ground. Grass for bedding was needed, but that would have to wait. They had promised Ulys they wouldn't leave the safety of the cavern, and it was a pledge.

Meanwhile, Buck and Ulys had moved down the hill to the relative safety of the trees. Their plan was to explore the tree line and, as they worked their way around the barren crags from the relative safety of the trees, to observe and study the rocky face of the mountain above them.

They started along the same path they had journeyed on to reach the cavern with the squirrels but soon turned in the opposite direction, all the while remaining within the protective shelter of the trees. They moved slowly and quietly, as they no longer had the luxury of the squirrels to warn them of danger. Ulys reflected that they would have to immediately start Buck on exercises to strengthen his forelegs and have him begin climbing the evergreens that were all around them. When Chatter returned, he could sharpen Buck's claws, and soon he, too, would be able to climb to escape dangers. For now, secrecy and speed were their best defenses.

The tree line proved interesting. There were many small caves or indentations in the rocky soil. Most were big enough for a rabbit to squeeze into, and this source of ready shelter was a great comfort to them both. As they proceeded, they marked areas like this with urine to help them find their way back quickly by their sense of smell, if need be.

Above them, on the bare mountain face, trickled many small, cold streams. The water was delicious, but very different from that found inside their cave. None of these streams sent columns of mist into the cool spring air.

Several times the rabbits were startled by the sounds of rocks falling from the slopes above. As they looked up the slope in terror each time, searching for the source of the noise, they realized it was only the sun, warming the soil, that had dislodged the rocks. None of the small slides carried rocks as far as the trees, but the adventurers remained wary.

Suddenly, the clear mountain air was torn by a harsh scream. Again, the two friends froze. Both knew it to be the cry of a raven, and while the raven was not a predator to them, the tone of the cry spoke of danger.

Ulys crept to the edge of the trees, unnerved by the continuing, strident cries. As he peeked up the mountain, a strange sight greeted his eyes.

A raven was sitting by the side of a stream, screaming loudly. He flopped and twisted, crying all the while. Finally Ulys realized what had caused this unusual scene. A rock slide, such as they had heard so often on this warm spring day, had trapped the raven, apparently as he stopped to drink from the stream. The bird grew more and more terrified, as it was unable to escape. He understood well enough that another animal would soon be along to make a meal of him if he were unsuccessful at freeing himself.

A week before, Ulys and Buck would have ignored the bird's plight. Its dilemma was the Creator's will and of no concern to them. But both had been changed by the ordeal they had been through. Without a sound being exchanged, they looked around for predators and, seeing none, proceeded together up the mountainside.

Their first priority was to calm the hysterical bird. Surely his strident cries would summon a predator, and soon. The next task was simple for the two digging animals. In a few minutes they had uncovered the trapped foot and wing of the great bird, and it hopped free.

It was only then that the large shadow passed over them. Both rabbits bolted for the safety of the trees. They had sensed the hawk, and in the open he was more than a match for them. Once sheltered by the trees, they would be safe from this danger at least. As they reached the trees, they thought of the raven. They turned and looked back to the mountain face. To their shock, they saw he hadn't flown to safety, but instead stood, braced unsteadily on one foot, and faced the hawk.

The two friends could now see what, in their haste to flee from the danger of the hawk, they had overlooked. Not only was the black bird's foot injured, but the wing feathers on the same side were bent. He was unable to run or fly. There was no way for him to escape, so he had turned and bravely faced the hawk. As the hawk swooped down to finish off his prey, he was greeted by a savage peck to his face that drew blood and sent him screaming into the sky.

The hawk temporarily dealt with, the raven began to hobble toward the safety of the trees. Again, with no signal, the two rabbits left their own shelter and went to the aid of the stricken bird.

The hawk circled in confusion. He had been hurt badly by his prey and was terribly confused by the unlikely reappearance of the two rabbits. Before he could clear his mind in these troubling circumstances, the three had reached the safety of the trees, and his chance for an easy meal had disappeared with them.

17
lord heat

The three escapees huddled under a spreading pine, shaken by their recent brush with death. The raven spoke first, in the sharp, strident tones of his kind. He thanked the two brave rabbits for attempting to help him, but assured them it hadn't been necessary. He had had that hawk right where he wanted him.

Ulys and Buck smiled. Tongues firmly in cheeks, they asked him to explain his terrible cries that had summoned both them and the bird of prey.

With great dignity, the raven smoothed his feathers and explained that the cries they had heard were merely the raven's way of summoning his strength before making good his escape. One who flew (like a god) needed no help from anyone who burrowed in the earth.

Ulys shrugged his ears and bid the raven good day. He was quite amused by the bird's silly explanation of the recent past events, now that his own fears had subsided. However, it was past time for them to return to the cavern. As the rabbits began to hop away, they were stopped by the loud cries of the bird himself. Despite his arrogant words, he was unable to fly and scarcely able to hop. A night on the ground in the forest would be his certain death warrant. The proud bird reluctantly asked the two for their assistance.

It was a strange sight that greeted Megan and Rachel at the mouth when the two explorers returned. The injured bird attempted to enter the cavern with dignity but tripped on his injured leg and tumbled into their midst, amid harsh bird screams of both pain and embarrassment.

The two startled does froze and trembled with terror until Buck and Ulys hurried in to explain. Rachel recovered quickly and ordered the others to help the injured bird down to the stream. She examined the damaged foot and told the raven to place his foot in the warm water of the spring. She quickly buried the injured extremity in a carefully prepared mixture of mud and moss to facilitate its healing.

She examined the injured wing with care. She soon realized that the wing itself was fine, but several of the large guard feathers were so badly bent that the wing was rendered useless. She told the raven the damaged feathers had to be removed. He, in turn, accepted the diagnosis calmly. The mud and moss had already worked enough to relieve much of the pain in his foot. He advised Rachel that, if need be, he could extricate the damaged feathers himself, with his own beak, but that the pain of such a procedure would leave him weak and ill for some time.

Megan had observed quietly until now. At this time, she suggested that the rabbits try to chew the feathers off, above the tender skin, to reduce the pain and damage to the raven. It was agreed to make this attempt, and Megan, having the daintiest mouth, was elected to perform the delicate procedure.

The raven was stoic as Megan gently cut through the damaged plumage. When finally the operation was complete, the raven collapsed in relief and joy. He could sense immediately that the wing had been restored to proper functioning.

The four rabbits left the raven, his foot still in the healing poultice, for their evening feed. As they fed on the mountainside's tender growth, Ulys recounted to them how this strange relationship had begun, explaining at great length how the hawk had been defeated by the courage of his intended victim. They gathered seeds for their feathered guest and returned to the cavern.

The raven ate greedily and without a word. When all they gathered had been consumed, he sat back, his injured foot still soaking in the soothing stream. Quietly he thanked them all. He was at a loss to explain their help, so uncommon in nature and indeed so unrabbitlike, but he knew he owed them his very life. He would, he assured them, find ways to repay his debt.

It was then that Xan choose to return up the passage. He crawled quietly into the cavern and was greeted by the outraged cries of the injured raven, who leaped from the stream, past the startled rabbits, and began to rain blows on the poor old reptile.

Ulys and Buck subdued the raven and recounted the strange tale of the stone-toothed creature. Even Xan, now recovered from this strange onslaught, was impressed by the courage the bird had shown, however misdirected. Slowly he regained his temper, never far from being unleashed. His rattles grew quiet, to the relief of all the assembled company. Finally, Xan asked the raven what his name was.

"I am the Lord Heat," spoke the raven. "I am master of all the birds on this mountain. Today, as my friends, your future has been assured! On this mountain, all that fly obey my command, except for the terrible birds of prey. They will listen to no one. But who has not seen groups of the common and lowly sparrows drive the great hawk from his nest?" said Heat, warming to his task.

He went on to explain that, by helping each other, the smaller birds were indeed able to survive on the mountain and enjoy its beauty and ride its strong winds. The great birds of prey were their own masters, and it was their independence and lack of cooperation that allowed the weaker birds to survive among their much stronger and more fierce brethren.

Ulys sat a moment in silence. Only his eyes showed that, for him, this was a moment of epiphany.

He then hurriedly began to explain to the assembled group—rabbits, reptile, and bird—his sudden vision. He believed that Heat had described how they must live if they hoped to survive the harsh mountain life.

He stated eloquently that, despite the legends of the Great Rabbit and the Creator, which said that every animal was the enemy of the rabbit, they must find a way to live and work together with the creatures around them. Cooperation among the predators' victims was imperative to assure their mutual survival.

His clan was skeptical. All knew, almost from birth, that rabbits lived alone, that fear and fleeing were the essential components to their survival. To counter this argument, Ulys pointed silently around the room. He reminded them of the service and the sacrifices of their brave squirrel friends. Slowly, all of them, reptile and bird as well, began to share this vision and his enthusiasm.

Heat, in his outspoken way, said he was sure the raptors that preyed on his kingdom would never coexist in peace with their weaker brethren. Ulys pointed to old Xan, and Heat was forced into silence.

Buck and Megan protested against what they had always known, the ways taught by the Great Rabbit and his legends. Ulys said that he felt they had all been led here by the paw of the Great Rabbit. Maybe the time had come for the ways of the rabbit and all other animals to change.

Lost, confused, and excited by the words spoken, each of the cavern's inhabitants sought his bed. All were fatigued by the events of the day, yet for all sleep was long in coming. Each asked in his or her own fashion whether this could be the beginning of a new way. Was there some greater meaning in their lonely struggle to survive?

Rachel lay longest before she slept. Ulys's strange words had thrilled her, and she sensed a great truth. One thing she knew for certain: four rabbits were not a clan. On the mountain, their little group needed more members if they hoped to survive.

18
down the mountain

The morning that greeted them was the most beautiful they had yet seen on the mountain. Summer was soon to be with them in earnest, and this day carried its promise.

Megan stood her turn as guard as all the inhabitants of the cave enjoyed the beauty of the mountainside on this pristine morning.

Heat had recovered enough to join them outside, and after a little practice, he found he could fly perfectly well, despite the necessary alterations of his wing feathers. He still limped heavily, but was able to move about well enough.

Xan was shown where the seeds and plants he now fed on grew. He couldn't eat them without the rabbits chewing them for him, but the old snake enjoyed the warmth of the sunshine and pointed out to the rabbits his favorite seeds. He would have preferred to be hunting, not gathering, but as his mouth healed, he accepted his fate rather well. This adjustment may have been partly due to his advanced age. The hunt grew more difficult with each year, and he secretly doubted he would have survived another dying season, were it not for the help of his new companions.

The rabbits talked excitedly about Ulys's statement of the night before. Each had thought long and hard about his strange and troubling words. They weren't sure exactly what these statements portended, but the ideas Ulys had expressed filled them with excitement.

Rachel shared her feelings about their need for more rabbits if they hoped to become a real clan. All agreed but were at a loss as to how to proceed with such a task. At the old warren, an occasional rabbit had found the dens and became a part of the clan, but such events were few and far between. On the mountain, above the tree line, the chance of any rabbit just wandering in was remote.

Buck suggested they go down below to search for additional members of their group. He hoped their squirrel friends could help in the effort. Ulys had no better plan, but was aware of how dangerous such a trip was for the nonclimbers. There was a real risk of losing an existing clan member in their attempt to expand their numbers.

It was Heat who provided the answer. He had been uncharacteristically quiet, but was listening intently to the discussion. He felt the debt he owed his new friends deeply and volunteered to have all of his many bird subjects search the area around them for possible rabbits to join the tiny clan.

The news was greeted with delight, but Ulys quickly calmed and quieted them. He said they were not yet ready for his search to occur. Too much still needed to be done to make the cavern into a true home for rabbits.

Rachel agreed. This was a subject in her area of expertise. She immediately directed Ulys and Buck to begin gathering food and bedding for their homes. She and Megan were to finish digging and lining the dens for the four. Xan could continue to gather seeds for himself and enjoy the sun, while Heat tested his wings and stood guard over them all while they worked.

And so the next several days went. Finally Rachel was satisfied. Their dens were completed and lined. They would be comfortable in any weather. They had even marked out the locations for several new dens, should their search yield new clan members.

A large amount of food for both them and Xan had been stored. Xan found that if the grain was carefully chewed in advance for him, he could now eat it without being fed. By now, Heat's wing was fine and his foot had almost healed.

It was time for their search for more members to begin. Heat set off to organize his flying friends, while all four of the rabbits began the journey back to the squirrels' hickory grove. No rabbits would be found on the mountain, so the cave was temporarily abandoned, and the easier downhill journey began.

Chatter and his clan were delighted to greet their friends. The squirrels had mourned the loss of their kinsman, but none had blamed the rabbits for the sad event.

Buck had been doing his climbing exercises, and even Rachel and Megan had joined him. Now, with help from their squirrel friends, they all had their toenails reshaped and began climbing practice in earnest.

The squirrels had worked to enlarge their visitors' scrape under the fragrant bush, and Rachel now lined it with soft grass. It wasn't as safe as the cave, but with the squirrels to guard them at night, it made an acceptable dwelling, even if not as warm and dry as the cavern.

In two days, Heat returned. The squirrels had heard the story of his rescue and friendship with the rabbits, but when he arrived in their hickory grove, along with ten of his noisy raven friends, it still caused quite a stir, even among the adventurous squirrel clan.

When everyone quieted down, Heat hopped to the floor of the hickory grove and, drawing himself up to his full stature and dignity, gave his report.

Indeed, he and his band had found rabbits. Most were too far away for the tiny clan to risk traveling to, but even as they spoke, a sorry-looking group of six rabbits was journeying just a few hills away. There had been seven the day before, but a dog had gotten one of the group, and the rest had fled in such terror that they were now exhausted and confused.

They were led by a buck named Jonar. Heat had followed them for a while to plot their journey's path. He knew they were fleeing from something, but they didn't seem to have a specific goal or destination in mind. Heat could guide them to the wandering group that very day if they wished.

One of Heat's subjects also had a story of great interest. There was trouble in the old warren, just down the hill. The new Lord had not grown in popularity since they had departed. Friends of Rachel, Buck, and Megan in particular had been angered by the Lord and many of his foolish decisions. They had begun to see him as both vain and foolish, two exceedingly dangerous traits in any leader.

The guard rabbits still kept order in the warren, being as fierce as they wished in demanding obedience, but the bird had overheard complaints as the rabbits fed.

Ulys decided Rachel and Buck should go to the old warren and try to determine exactly what state it was in. He doubted they would be in any danger, as they had not been banished as he had, but rather had left of their own choosing. Still, he cautioned them to listen in silence before they approached within range of the guards. He had an uneasy feeling about the warren, but trusted Buck with Rachel's safety.

Ulys and Megan were going to leave at once to intercept the group of rabbits traveling their way. Some of the ravens would accompany each group. Ulys asked Heat to stay with Buck and Rachel, and his friend agreed. Chatter and his cousin, despite the terrible loss of their kinsman before, insisted on joining Ulys and Megan on their adventure. The other squirrels promised to keep an eye on happenings around the old warren.

There was a lot of nose touching, even with the squirrels, before the separation. The much-amused ravens looked on. At last Ulys and Megan turned to follow the ravens, with Chatter and friend in the trees above them. Rachel and Buck quietly turned toward their old home, accompanied by several squirrels. Heat and his friends flew ahead to position themselves above the rabbits and wait for Megan and Ulys to join them.

19
the clan grows

Ulys and Megan moved quickly through the forest. With the squirrels and now the ravens to watch over them, they had little cause to feel fearful during their journey. That was especially true as now Megan could at least climb an evergreen tree to avoid danger.

Following their raven guides, they soon found the wandering band of six rabbits. They did indeed look worn and defeated. They had dug a shallow scrape under a bush, but it offered little protection, comfort, or safety for the little group. They appeared too defeated and exhausted to continue to travel.

The six seemed too tired even to feed and just sat in the wet grass, shaking and barely able to move. Both Megan and Ulys recognized the effects sheer terror had on rabbits in their trembling bodies. Even their fur, dirty and torn, showed signs of the strain.

Ulys could see their leader, the one Heat had called Jonar, standing guard over the clan. He, too, looked exhausted, yet there still burned in his eyes a light of defiance. He was a large, well-built male, who wore the scars of old battles in several places on his muscular body. Obviously worn and tired, he just as clearly wasn't defeated.

Ulys and Megan planned to spend the night in a pine tree and approach the clan in the morning, after they had some time to rest and be refreshed. Ulys would first learn their situation, then invite the six to come and stay in the cavern.

But the harsh warning cry of one of their raven friends changed all their plans. The cry was to alert them to the presence of a dog creeping up on the exhausted group. Ulys sensed in a minute that it was the very canine that had destroyed one of their band before. The tired six reacted to the cry of the bird by huddling in fear and confusion near the worthless scrape, too tired to flee. They sensed danger but didn't know of what kind or from where it came.

Jonar rallied them. He soon had the five rabbits in the scrape, while he remained outside. Ulys at once saw his plan. He would lead whatever threatened them away from the rest of the clan to assure their safety.

Ulys also saw that in Jonar's present condition, the chase could only end in his death cry. It took only an instant for Ulys to read all this from the situation, but by the time that instant had ended, the dog was upon Jonar.

Ulys yelled at Chatter and his cousin to get Megan safely into a tree. He asked the ravens to follow him and then set out at an angle that would allow him to intersect the fleeing dog and rabbit. He ran like the wind, his powerful back legs eating up the distance so quickly that he outdistanced even the ravens. He crested a small rise and almost collided with a stunned Jonar. Ulys changed directions quickly and ran right in front of the dog, now just a few short feet behind the exhausted rabbit.

The dog veered instinctively to follow this new closer prey. It never expected or understood what happened next. Ulys ran on a few yards farther to put some distance between himself and his pursuer. As he ran, he searched and soon saw what he needed—a large hickory tree. He veered directly toward it and, still at top speed, ran a few feet up the trunk.

The poor dog adjusted his path to intercept his new quarry, but ran directly into the tree. In his astonishment and rage, he jumped to catch the rabbit in his sharp teeth. Instead, he got both sets of Ulys's sharp back claws in his nose. The blood flow blinded him, and at that instant the five ravens descended upon him.

Thinking the hounds of hell themselves were on his heels, the dog fled, howling, tail between his legs, over the hillside.

As Ulys leaped nimbly to the ground, he heard a strange sound. It was Jonar, and the sound was his laughter. The excitement and terror of the chase, plus the strange fate that had befallen the dog, had overcome him completely. He rolled on the ground in complete, helpless, and uncontrollable spasms of mirth.

Ulys was at first concerned. Was this the final stage of the terror syndrome that would lead to death? Finally, he realized the humor was healthy, and thinking of the scene the dog had made as he exited the field with his vanguard of ravens, he soon joined Jonar in his laughter.

No words were exchanged as the two, by common desire, returned to their respective friends. Slowly the five moved from the scrape, completely puzzled by what little they had seen of the event. Where was the dog? What was so funny? Who was this big buck with the funny ears and long legs?

Ulys and Jonar could only laugh harder as the questions poured from the group. Finally, Megan and her two squirrel friends returned, along with the ravens. At last Ulys was able to control his humor and speak.

"Fellow rabbits, night will soon be upon us. It is not a safe time for rabbits to stray from the mouth of the warren. If you will join us, we have a den a few hours from here that will shelter you all. There is food and water enough for your needs. I know you have many questions, and they will be answered, but the time and place now are too dangerous to allow delay."

Jonar spoke in return, "Friend, you have saved my life—you and your companions. The Great Rabbit must have sent you, and we will follow. Lead us to safety and then we will talk."

Ulys made a signal, and the squirrels and ravens returned to guard duty. The group struck a course up the mountain, toward the cavern. Ulys and Megan led, and the whole party moved quickly through the forest, their fears and fatigue almost forgotten with the promise of shelter, food, and safety. When they reached the tree line, some of the six hesitated, but Jonar pushed on and the others quickly followed. Soon they all arrived at the mouth. The ravens left, to cries of thanks, to roost among the trees and tell stories of their successful attack on the dog. The squirrels and rabbits were soon in the strange den.

As the six fed on the stored food and drank the water, even washing their wounds in the healing springs, Ulys and Megan told their story. By the time they got to Xan, the other rabbits were so amazed at what they had heard that the existence of a large rattlesnake in the den seemed to bother them little. Had Ulys not proved much of what he said by his actions, he would have been taken for a fool by all in the group.

Finally, the story told, the rabbits all sat in silent wonder and contemplated the amazing tale they had heard. Then Jonar began his story.

The six at one time had been nine. Three of their members had been lost to predators on their journey. The survivors had given up all hope of finding a new warren and waited, in rabbitlike fashion, to offer up their death cries to the Great Rabbit.

The journey had started with the banishment of the nine

from a warren some distance from Rachel's old home. The Lord Rabbit of their warren had banished them in a dispute over feeding grounds. Their warren was so large that feeding areas were assigned and the assignments enforced by the guards. Their group had been given the worst feed, at the greatest distance from the safety of the mouth.

Two of the rabbits at this feed had already been lost to predators when the group had approached the Lord. Their request was simple—that the feeding ground assignments be rotated among all the members of the warren. They would take their turn at this plot but felt it was unfair to be forced to feed there forever.

The Lord had flown into a rage. He felt his word and decisions were being questioned. He forbade them to ever leave the grounds to which they had been assigned, on pain of banishment. The next day Jonar led eight of his friends to another field to feed. They were banished from the warren at once, and roughly so, by the guard rabbits who had been warned of just such a possibility.

The days that followed had been hard. Jonar was brave—none would question that—but he had no plan. His only hope was to keep moving and hope the Great Rabbit would intervene on their behalf. He felt the appearance of Ulys and Megan at such a critical time was, indeed, by the hand of the Great Rabbit himself.

Ulys and Megan were a little taken aback to be seen as emissaries from the gods. Yet they saw at once that these poor pilgrims were exactly what they needed to form a true warren. They were young, strong, and brave enough to stand up and question their leaders. True, ten was not enough for a real warren, but it was better—much better than four. The stories completed, all lay down to sleep. In the morning they had already planned to begin to dig their new dens. Ulys's thoughts now turned to Buck, Rachel, and Heat. He wondered what they had found at the old warren.

20
the old warren

Rachel and Buck approached the old warren cautiously. Neither could say exactly why, but both felt apprehensive about going "home" again. Heat flew on ahead and was positioned over them in a tree as they cautiously crept near enough to the warren to observe its activity. Things looked the same. Their old friends were feeding and visiting near the mouth, just as they had done in years past. It was all Rachel could do not to run down and greet them.

But Buck was very concerned with his responsibilities as leader and protector, and he cautioned Rachel to remain silent and continue to observe. Still, from what Buck could see, there was no danger. Everything looked tranquil.

Suddenly a rabbit's scream was heard. Both Rachel and

Buck looked in the direction of the disturbance. They saw a young rabbit, with its shoulder bleeding badly, being pulled aside by a guard rabbit. It took them a moment to realize that the guard had caused the serious wound.

As the two neared the mouth, the guard spoke so all the clan could hear.

"This foolish one strayed from the area allowed. You see how he has been punished? The Lord Rabbit will extract even more in payment. Let this stupid one's fate be a lesson to all of you."

Several of the rabbits who had been in the area of the injured youngster were returning to the den, visibly shaken.

Rachel heard one of the rabbits say, "He's just a lad, and he wandered a bit too far in his youth. Why should he be punished so terribly for such a small thing? By what right?"

Other rabbits hurried to stop the conversation, but it was too late. A guard had overheard and moved in on the doe. With a vicious butt he moved her toward the mouth.

"No one may question the Lord's laws," he said.

Rachel and Buck watched in horror. Even Heat let out a cry of anger. But the other rabbits continued to feed with their heads down. Now no one spoke.

As the feeding time ended, the rabbits made their way slowly, seemingly reluctantly, to the mouth. Near the end of the procession was an old doe who had been Rachel's friend all of their years together in the warren. Without a word to Buck, Rachel kicked a pebble toward her. When the doe looked up, Rachel leaned forward and motioned for her to come. Head still down, the old doe worked her way toward a large bush and, under its cover, waited until all the other warren members were inside. Then she ran quickly to meet her old friend.

Polly touched noses with Rachel. She was delighted to see her old friend still alive. She was also surprised, as all knew that to leave the clan meant certain death.

Polly signaled that she couldn't talk there. Buck led them quietly off toward the hickories. Heat watched to be sure they weren't followed.

At last, Polly felt safe. She again touched noses with Rachel and Buck and then started to weep. Slowly, haltingly, the story of the warren came out. The new Lord was harsh. He demanded strict obedience to his word, or punishment was unmerciful. The warren had become a house of terror to many, yet none dared to protest. To do so meant banishment and death. It seemed the punishment of Ulys, and the desertion of the three who chose to follow him, had enraged the Lord. In response to this self-perceived threat to his authority, more and stricter laws were developed and vigorously enforced.

Polly was quite upset from the telling of the tale. The two punished today had been her friends. Free from the constraints of the warren, she broke down and sobbed. Buck and Rachel escorted her to the hickory grove of the squirrels. She was amazed to find a safe den there and to discover the friendship between her friends and the squirrels.

As the night passed, Buck and Rachel described to the amazed Polly the events that had occurred since they had left the warren only a few short weeks before. The idea of a cavern in the mountains was beyond Polly's imagination, but she could imagine life with her old friends, away from the warren and its ubiquitous rules.

The two friends assured her she was welcome to join them in their new-found haven. Polly tearfully replied that she couldn't leave her children, no matter how bad things were. Rachel and Buck understood. Once again it was Heat who formulated a plan.

The three rabbits were near the big bush, the very one where Ulys had saved Megan what now seemed a lifetime ago, when morning dawned. Slowly, the warren rabbits came out to feed. Polly's children, all eight of them, had missed her the night before. They were furious that they weren't allowed to go and search for her immediately, but the guards had forbidden it. Now all eight wandered together in search of their mom. The anger that radiated from them as a group assured that no guard would bother them, even if they broke one of the innumerable rules.

As they neared the bush hiding place of our heroes, Heat went into action. He swooped low over the rabbits and right into the mouth itself. Before the stunned guards could react, he hopped away, with the startled guards in pursuit.

With the guards thus distracted, Polly jumped up and called to her children. They ran to her, overjoyed that she was safe. She quickly told them they were to follow her. She had no time to explain. Rachel led them all back to the den in the hickories.

The guards soon gave up chasing the foolish raven, who cawed down derisively after them from his safe perch in a tall tree. When they realized that the other rabbits had left their area, an alarm was sounded and they hurried in pursuit. As the guards reached the infamous bush, the lead rabbit was suddenly sent tumbling down the bank. Buck had delivered a kick that would have made Ulys proud. Now all the ravens started to swoop down and shriek at the guard rabbits. In the confusion that followed, Buck made a hasty retreat toward the shelter of the hickories.

Polly's family had not been long in the den, rejoicing at their mom's safety and seeing their old friends, when the ravens and squirrels set up a real fuss. Buck peered out of the den to see the guards approaching, now reorganized and led by the Lord himself. They had stopped at the edge of the hickories, confused by the ravens and squirrels, yet determined to re-capture the fleeing rabbits.

Buck strode out bravely to confront them. There were twenty guards, but Buck was unafraid. There were over one hundred squirrels, and Buck knew of their sharp teeth, lightning quickness, and ferocious natures.

The Lord drew himself up, both in dignity and anger. He demanded the rabbits return at once, or he would banish them from the warren on the spot.

Polly heard this statement and stepped forth. She told the Lord that in her many years she had never been treated so terribly as she had during the time of his rule. She also told him that she and hers would not return to the warren. All the assembly laughed loudly when she told the Lord that her family was banishing him from them.

The Lord was furious. He glared at the rebellious doe, but she stared fixedly back. He thought to order his guards to seize the two and deal with the menacing squirrels as best they could. As he raged and thought, Buck climbed a tree. The guards looked on in shock and horror. Buck plucked a green hickory nut and threw it down at the astonished guard rabbits. Soon the squirrels followed suit. Even the ravens rained nuts on the Lord and his guards. The proud Lord fled in complete disarray as the rabbits cheered.

The next morning, the whole troop made their way to the cavern. Ulys and Megan were delighted to see Rachel and Buck return with their old friend Polly and her wonderful family. Introductions to Jonar and his band were soon made. It took a little longer for them to greet Xan, who was almost as upset by all the strangers as they were by his presence. He retreated quickly down the passage, to the relief of the new members of the clan.

After breakfast on the mountain face and a time of rest and catching up among the group, everyone pitched in and the next few days were busy with dens being dug and grass and seeds being harvested. It was several days before all were settled in their new homes and the four who began the great adventure had time to talk.

Ulys listened to Buck and Rachel's tale. He had no love for the Lord, but was saddened to think of rabbits forced to live as those in his old warren and Jonar's were being forced to exist. He thought long and hard about the situation. Was it true that only complete obedience, even to the point of accepting death, was essential to the survival of rabbits? Ulys couldn't agree in his heart, but who was he to defy the ways of rabbits? Maybe it was the troubled mind he fell asleep with, but whatever the cause, that night he had a dream that changed his life, and the lives of all around him, forever.

21
ulys's dream

The dream was of his mother, whom Ulys had never really seen, at least with earthly eyes. Yet in the dream he saw her—young, brave, and beautiful. Maybe she was blessed too richly by the gods, because as he watched her life unfold he saw great peaks of joy and great valleys of pain.

His mother had known great love, and maybe because of this she had not known fear. She had dared to live a life filled with joy, bowing to none. For her courage and beauty, she had been greatly loved. For the same strength, she had been greatly feared and hated.

All these things were plain to Ulys as he slept. They could be seen simply by watching her play on a dreamy, sunlit meadow. Yet, for his poor mother, even the brightest of suns seemed to hold dark clouds.

She had not just questioned authority. She had done much worse. She had lived her life as if no authority existed. She had dared to choose joy in the place of misery. She had challenged life instead of accepting it. Much as the Great Rabbit in the Creation story, she lived every moment to the fullest. It was soon evident to those in power in her warren that she would have to be destroyed.

Ulys saw the reasons plainly. Those who preached of pain and fear as the rabbit's lot couldn't tolerate her lack of these feelings. A rabbit lived to be hunted. Fate, to them, was in acceptance of death. Life, such as it was, was a furtive, scary thing—always edged with disaster. One had to accept it as such. The leaders had rules and assistants to enforce these rules. They alone knew what was best for all. For the well-being of the clan, the laws had to be obeyed at all times and at all costs.

Joy led to carelessness, and carelessness led to death. Who could deny these facts of life? Only in fear could rabbits hope to survive. True, their lives were lived in dark, cold caves, hidden from the sun. But to abolish the fear would be the death of them all.

His mother had been scolded and cuffed since she was an infant, but to no avail. She was born into a world of wonder and joy—a world full of excitement. In this world there was great love and little fear. She cared for all others and tried to mind their instructions, but no effort seemed great enough to overcome her joy.

All this Ulys saw and knew to be true. As he dreamed, he saw clouds of danger build up all around her, as they had around him and Rachel. As they had been, she was helpless to avoid them.

But in his dream he also saw the Great Rabbit. Ulys saw him smile down with love and joy on his poor, doomed mother. Ulys saw him laugh with delight as she cavorted in the meadows, fearless in her bliss. He smiled knowingly at the little tricks she played on her friends and the laughter these escapades brought to all.

The Great Rabbit saw the dark clouds too, but he was not afraid. He seemed to say to Ulys that to play in joy and love was better than to hide, fearing the storm. Better to dare to live than to live in fear, even unto death. The Great One knew that death was not to be feared. What should strike terror was the choice of death during life.

This choice of a living death was the death that reigned eternal, as it was selected by the rabbits themselves. Why, wondered the Great Rabbit, could they not see the simple truth that life was a choice? Life gave in return whatever one asked from it. To live a life free of fear, one had simply to choose joy.

Now Ulys, in his sleep, was still. Had anyone observed him, they would have seen a smile play on his lips. He saw the clouds break. He saw the anger of the others who chose fear. He witnessed what they took to be his mother's destruction. Yet still he smiled.

He saw his mother now, and his five brothers and sisters, still filled with joy. Still playing in the sunlit fields. Still free of fear. Death had come to them, as it does to all. None can escape that fate. But fear is a choice made, one his mother never chose.

In his dream, Ulys's mother and siblings smiled on him, and he knew he need never fear again. He might win or he might lose in his battles with life, but Ulys knew he had only one decision in his life to make: to choose joy.

Ulys woke with the smile still on his lips. Unlike most dreams, this one stayed completely in his mind. He understood every part of the dream without knowing how. Lying quietly in his den, Ulys gazed back over his young life. His smile never wavered, because in all he had done, he had never lost joy. He was indeed his mother's son. He knew this meant dark clouds in his life. There had been many already. But through them all reigned the choice of joy.

Now he gazed ahead. In his mind he saw his tiny warren gathered round him in sleep. Slowly he thought of all of their pasts. Despite differences, and perhaps because of their differences, this group had come to be one. All their paths shared the same destination: a refusal to accept the life of fear and dread that was supposed to be their lot.

What did the choice of these few alone on this mountaintop mean? The mountaintop, treeless and wind swept, was a symbol of their freedom. The dark cave, so scary at first, had become a place of warmth, sharing, and love, but only after the great snake of their fears had been faced and made to do their bidding. Ulys saw that it wasn't a piece of stone that had tamed Xan to their will, but rather their need, their courage, and their decision to live with joy.

Could all such battles be won with such unsophisticated weapons as the love and commitment of this band to their common beliefs?

To this question Ulys had no answer. But a part of him knew that the question was pointless to ask. Only one question really meant anything: Am I moving toward my joy? This one inquiry easily contained all the other questions of life within it.

As Ulys lay wrapped in this warm blanket of thought, Rachel awoke. She too awoke with a smile. All her life she had felt the Great Rabbit near. Since Ulys had come into her life, changing it so completely, she had felt his divine presence in the young male. Because of this she had faced death for him. No vision had lain across her sleep. None was needed. Her life was spent giving to the ones she loved. Ulys was her joy. This was more than enough.

Slowly the cavern came to life. All in it seemed to feel the peace that had come upon them. As the warren fed in the early sunlight, Xan curled up on a rock nearby, and Heat circled noisily above, they all felt contentment and joy. None felt this great prize had been won by his or her personal courage. They had simply acted as they believed. The fact that these actions had meant that each of them faced death for his or her beliefs simply wasn't important. They had chosen life, even if doing so meant facing death. All understood that they had made what for them was the only possible choice. Each, in his or her own way, thanked the Great Rabbit for the courage that had been given them all.

22
return to the warren

Later that day, the four who started the grand adventure had time to talk. Since their move to the cave, Megan and Ulys had grown close. Soon, the first litter born to the new warren would be theirs. Rachel needed to find a new den for herself, but all would help to prepare it, and soon the warren would be filled with new life.

Buck, too, had taken a mate. It didn't seem like much time would be required for the size of the new clan to double. Xan and Heat both lived with them now, and no predator dared to attack. The constant fear of sudden death, which every rabbit was seemingly born with, was slowly falling away. Food was plentiful, and the den, now that they were used to it, was the most wonderful place any rabbit had ever lived. Even the harsh dying months held no fear for them now, thanks to the cavern and its warmth, water supply, and constant food.

Still, Ulys was not at ease. He couldn't erase the memory of the old warren, nor forget the pain of those still living there. Could he choose joy and not offer it to others? Yet the warren guards greatly outnumbered his small company. He faced great danger if he went among them, yet slowly he realized that go among them he must.

When he told the four of his decision to once again descend the mountain, none demurred. They knew they had been given a gift too great not to share. Somehow, this gift had to be extended to all.

Buck and Ulys set out at once for the hickory grove. Once in the trees, they traveled mostly in squirrel fashion. Both still practiced climbing regularly, and, while no rivals to the squirrels in ability, they could move well through the timber. Heat kept them company as they moved from branch to branch. Soon they were reunited with Chatter and his family. The night passed in the great joy of the friends' reunion.

Ulys had changed the lives of the squirrels too. Their beliefs were, and always had been, far different from those of the rabbits. They were all fiery fighters. Yet quietly they began to see in Ulys and his friends a greater strength. They were fascinated by their legends of the Creator. Little by little, they found themselves accepting, rather than fighting, all that life brought them.

None would refer to these fierce little creatures as mellow. They still teased the wolf as he walked through the forest. They still dared the eagle from their tree perches. Yet something had changed. In their lives were less fighting and battle and more quiet acceptance and joy. None could explain the change completely, not even Chatter. Yet all felt it, and with it had come a certain peace.

The squirrels listened to Buck and Ulys explain the reasons for their return to the old warren. Chatter and all his friends advised against such an undertaking. They felt that great danger, even death, awaited them at the hands of the embarrassed and enraged Lord.

At the very least, the squirrels wanted to be there to protect the two. Ulys and Buck refused their kind offer. They went to offer peace, not war, to their old friends. At first morning light, they journeyed down the hill to meet with the feeding rabbits of the warren.

The sight of the two caused a huge uproar among the members of the clan. The guards immediately sounded the alarm. More guards poured from the mouth, and they were soon followed by the Lord himself. Buck and Ulys waited quietly and calmly as the Lord approached.

"I see you have come to beg us to readmit all of you to the warren. I came myself to tell you that laws have been broken, and you must pay the price. You will find no mercy here," spoke the proud Lord.

Ulys responded, "We have come to offer mercy, not to seek it."

The whole warren had gathered around the guards and were stunned by Ulys's bold words.

Ulys went on to explain about the new warren. He told of the moss and the warm stream and of the protection of Heat above, which meant no guards were needed for their safety. He explained that in their warren none ruled and there were no laws. All were there because that was where their lives had taken them. It was their choice.

The Lord swelled up in a rage. "No laws indeed!" He cursed Buck and Ulys in the name of the Great Rabbit and ordered his guards to haul them away. Heat let out a great scream, and Chatter and his friends, who had crept up behind unbeknownst to Ulys, cried out too. None were close enough to save the two from their fate.

But the rabbits of the warren were. Every single one turned on the guards. The guards were unceremoniously driven from the scene in minutes, and a roar of triumph rose up from the rabbits, squirrels, and Heat as well.

Ulys went at once to the Lord. He told him that he and his guards were still welcome in the new warren, but that their power was not. But these men, too, had made a choice—one of fear—and, in their minds, it was too late for them to turn back. Instead, they would remain behind, alone in the old warren.

Much remains of the legend. The warren grew, as did the legend of the strange creatures who lived there. Many animals of various kinds came to the cavern, drawn by a mysterious force. Those who journeyed there were made welcome. Some chose to stay. No matter what their species, the animals who chose to reside on the mountain were those who celebrated a oneness in Creation...who had made a choice for joy and against fear...who realized the excitement of the future was that they were free to choose.